CRAFTING WITH SLANDER

Gasper's Cove Mysteries Book 3

BARBARA EMODI

C&T PUBLISHING
Another Maker Inspired!

Gasper's Cove Mysteries Series

DEDICATION

*To my mother-in-law Rose,
a DeWolf original.*

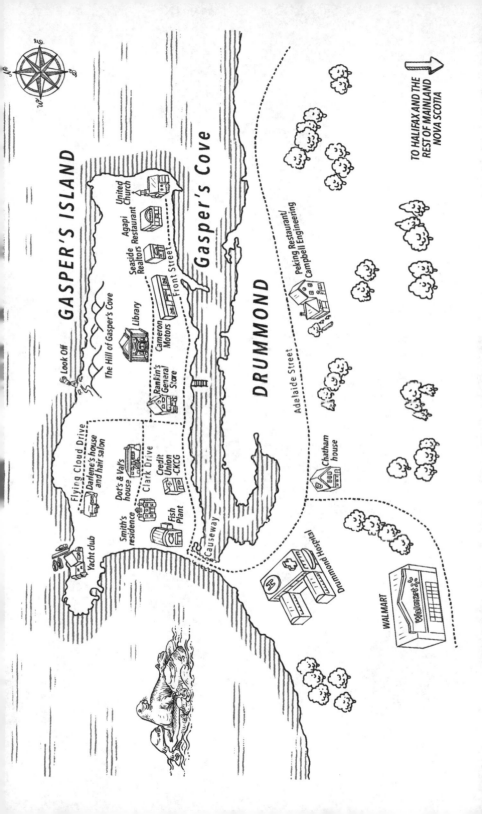

CHAPTER ONE

"Who has some dynamite? We've got to blow up the causeway."

Annette LeBlanc slammed her phone down onto the Co-op counter "Time we cut them off," she said.

"Dynamite? Where are we going to get that?" I asked. I saw that the screen of her phone was now cracked. "Be practical."

Annette stared at me while she thought. "Can't you make explosives yourself? I remember something about baking soda and vinegar ... "

"That's for sinks," I reminded her. "For a big explosion, you need the real stuff." I refocused. "But hang on. Why are we doing this?"

Sylvie interrupted before Annette could answer.

"If we can't get explosives, how about a human chain?" she asked. Sylvie picked up the phone and read. "We can hold hands and block the road. No one gets in or out."

Annette shook her head, bouncing the beach waves of her blond wig. "We can't do that. My kids' orthodontist is in Drummond."

Sylvie considered this setback. "How about a giant knitted barrier with a button-up gate for emergencies? We could use up all that cheap acrylic." She had once yarn-bombed the parking meters downtown with hand-knitted scarves. A graduate of the Nova Scotia College of Art and Design, Sylvie was a high-concept thinker.

But I was the manager. And we were crafters, not terrorists. "Give me that phone," I said, prying it out of Sylvie's hand. "What's going on?"

As soon as I saw the headline, I knew.

The Towns of Gasper's Cove and Drummond to Merge
Mayor Mike Murphy Seals the Deal

I could smell coconut hand cream behind me. My cousin Darlene had moved in to read over my shoulder.

"That man lies like a carpet," she sputtered. "He said it wouldn't happen." The coffee in Darlene's hand splashed onto a display of stained-glass suncatchers. I reached for a paper towel. Darlene was on the Gasper's Cove town council. If a merger was in the works, she would know.

I sighed. The clean-up session I'd organized with the Co-op's crafters was over. Dusters were down, outrage was up.

"Look what happened when they joined Musquodoboit with the Harbor." An older volunteer's voice shook. "It was a disaster."

The room agreed. They'd heard the stories and repeated them now.

"Seniors couldn't pay the new taxes. Lost their houses."

"Cars got $50 tickets for parking on the street in a snowstorm."

"The school closed."

"It killed the place."

"Turned Musquodoboit into a donut town. Good stuff on the edges. Hole in the middle."

"They merge us, and the Agapi restaurant will be gone."

"Put in an Olive Garden instead."

"Replace this store with a Walmart."

"Can't do that, this is a heritage property."

"All right then, they'd build a Walmart next door, just as bad."

The group went silent. The Crafters' Co-op was on the second floor of my family business, Rankin's General, on Front Street, Gasper's Cove, Nova Scotia. The store, like the street, hadn't changed in 120 years.

"Mike can't do this," I argued. "Who gave him the right?"

"Those idiots at Province House, that's who," Darlene snapped. "The stupid government is offering $200,000 to municipalities willing to absorb smaller communities. The province is calling it *rationalization*."

"Mike sold us out? For money?" I was shocked. I knew the mayor of Drummond. "Mighty Mike" Murphy was a classic back-slapping rural politician. Up to now, I had considered him harmless. "He can't do that. We're different towns," I said.

Annette took her phone back. "That could change." She started to read out loud. "Listen to this."

> As directed by the province, amalgamation can occur after a joint municipal election. The new councils would then decide whether they want to proceed as one or two towns. In a surprise move, Mayor Murphy has called for an election to accelerate the process of joining the communities.
>
> "I know what people want," Murphy said. "Let the people vote. They'll get behind whatever I think is best. You're looking at the next mayor of a bigger, better, stronger municipality. Good as a done deal."
>
> When asked by reporters what the expanded town would be called, Mayor Murphy said his preference would be DUM, Drummond United Municipality. Pressed on what the citizens of Gasper's Cove would think of the new name, Mayor Murphy's response was definitive.
>
> "They'll get used to it."

By the time Annette had finished reading, Darlene's face was as red as her hair. I could see the wheels whirling behind my cousin's blue eyes. I held my breath. What Darlene said next would be significant. She was as close to a real politician as anyone we knew.

"You know what this means?" she asked us. We didn't, but waited to find out. "Once an election is called, the whole council is disbanded. That's the system. Everything will be up to the new council and the new mayor. We need someone who won't let this happen to run against Mike."

"Maybe, what's-his-name Nickerson," I suggested. "The senator's son. I heard he's interested in the mayor's job. He might knock out Mike."

"Nickerson?" Darlene bristled. "Don't trust him. He's a bigger-is-better kind of guy."

"It's out of our hands then," Annette said. "Who else is there?"

I had a queasy feeling in my stomach. I was afraid of what was coming next.

"Me," Darlene said. "I will."

I took off my work apron and put it on the hook behind the counter. I moved slowly as I tried to put together the right words. Darlene wasn't up to this challenge. Couldn't she see that?

"Look, you are an excellent hair stylist and great crocheter," I began. I pointed to a display of her potholders as proof. "Besides, they already made you town councillor for this part of the island," I reminded her. "Mayor of the whole thing is different."

"Different? How?" Darlene asked. I knew that testy tone. I looked around to the rest of the group for support.

"To run for mayor, you need big money and connections," Annette said, backing me up. "You need signs. You need buttons. You need speeches. You need workers." She put her hand on Darlene's shoulder and shook it, as if trying to jiggle in some common sense. "Think about it. You don't have any of that. Dynamite would be easier."

"We are talking about being taken over by *Drummond*." Darlene moved out from under Annette's hand. "You know what they're like."

We knew.

Only ten minutes apart, Gasper's Cove, Nova Scotia (population 2,000) had absolutely nothing in common with Drummond (population 5,000). Over here, we had history, craftspeople, and artists. Over there, on the other side of the causeway, they had an outlet store, a call center, and a tire plant. Even worse, for decades, the citizens of Drummond had called us the Last Gaspers from Last Gasp. If they thought we hadn't heard them, they were wrong.

I knew when I was defeated. Darlene had been standing up to bullies ever since we were kids.

"I've got an idea for signs," one of our members said, breaking the silence. "Stencils. I did a border on a bedroom once. It's not hard." A couple of her friends nodded; stenciling had been big in the 1990s. Many of them still had the brushes down in the basement.

Our best baby-clothes knitter, Tilly Ferguson, put up her hand. Working small was her specialty. "What about campaign buttons?" she asked. "They'd be like coasters with a pin on the back. I could get the girls at church to start cross-stitching."

Darlene suddenly looked taller. "I can talk," she said. "I can make speeches. And for a campaign manager"—she elbowed me in the ribs—"I've got my relatives."

I didn't say anything. Instead, I moved away to the big semicircular window. I looked out over the water. I couldn't do it. I already managed a store, ran the Co-op, and was behind in my sewing. I wasn't even sure I had voted in the last election. I stalled. I pretended to admire the view.

On the street below, I saw a car towing a tent trailer pull up next to the wharf. Ontario plates. A young couple got out. The man was about the same age as my sons. I thought that

I recognized him—he must be home for a visit. Across from him, the young woman posed in front of a pile of lobster traps. The young man held up his phone and took a picture. The couple both studied the phone and laughed, no doubt posting for the benefit of friends in Toronto.

I remembered then that Darlene had come to the house to do my hair the morning after the last of my children left home. I turned around.

"If there's no one else," I said. "I'll do it. I'll try."

Darlene reached across the counter and crushed me in a hug. I could feel the relief in her body. Then, a shadow passed across her face.

"What will I wear?" she asked, stricken.

"I have your measurements," I reassured her. I sewed, she didn't. "We'll figure it out."

Across from us, Sylvie worked her way to the front of the group. She smelled strongly of fish. No wonder her seaweed cosmetics were hard to sell. "I'll help with the signs," she said. "But I have one question. What will they say?"

We looked at each other. Our minds went blank.

Then, it came to me like a vision. I could see it as if it were floating in the sky, above the waves. In big letters.

"DUM is DUMB," I blurted. "VOTE DARLENE."

There was silence while everyone considered this idea, then applause. I felt proud. I had coined my first political slogan.

"Perfect," Darlene said. It was done.

"Mighty Mike has no idea who he is dealing with," she whispered to me.

No, he didn't.

But neither did we.

CHAPTER TWO

The official launch of Darlene's campaign for mayor went well. We held it at the store. We served tea and oatcakes. We had dozens of signs. The production line running in the basement of my bungalow had outdone itself.

We knew what we were doing, after all.

Then, a journalist from the *Lighthouse Online* called.

That's when the trouble started. Nodding to me as her campaign manager, Darlene put her phone on speaker.

"This is a lifestyle piece," the young woman explained. "You know, a get-to-know-your-candidate sort of thing. Informal and fun. First question: What's your favorite color?"

"Turquoise. I'm a spring," Darlene answered, looking at the bright lettering on our signs. "I planned my signs to be like accessories. I don't want to clash."

"Okay," the reporter said slowly, as if taking notes. "Favorite band? Food? Dogs or cats?"

"The band would have to be Great Big Sea, lobster, and what was the last one?"

"Which do you like better, dogs or cats?"

Darlene didn't hesitate. "Cats. Definitely. I'm the original cat lady."

The reporter seemed pleased with this answer. "Great. Just what I was looking for. Got to jet, get this posted," she said abruptly.

Within an hour, the story was up.

Catty Candidate Disses Dogs

Social media exploded. Voters, mostly those on the Drummond side, posted pictures of dogs lifting their legs in front of our beautiful handmade signs. Hashtags tore around the internet: #nodognovote, #muzzledarlene, and the one that enraged me most, #barkformike.

I knew it. Mike Murphy was behind this article. No surprise there. I was the campaign manager. Damage control would be my first job. I'd make him stop. I'd have it out with him face-to-face at his campaign headquarters. I jumped in my car and headed across the causeway. The outgoing mayor wasn't getting away with this.

It wasn't hard to find the "Mike: Steady at the Helm" base of operations. It was back in the same rented space where it had been the last five elections, jammed in between the dry cleaners and the Foodmart in the Drummond strip mall. The windows of Mike's mission control center were plastered with bigger-than-life-size photos of the man himself. I noted that all had been shot from a low angle to make the mayor look taller and thinner than he really was.

Ignoring the sea of Mike faces, I tried the door. It was unlocked. I walked right in.

Whoa.

If this office was what a real campaign headquarters looked like, Darlene and I were in trouble.

Her campaign was being run from my living room, in the mid century modern house I had inherited from my aunt Dot.

We used a beige wall phone in the kitchen to make calls.

Mike had banks of phones in front of dozens of chairs for volunteers.

We folded our pamphlets on a kidney-shaped coffee table in front of a nubby green nylon couch.

Mike's HQ had four rows of tables, three photocopiers, and a stand for two coffee urns. His team had real office furniture, even chairs with all the wheels.

Our team worked on tin TV trays decorated with scratched mallard ducks, sat on hassocks with frayed piping, and ate baking brought from home. Darlene sat with us on the floor and stuffed envelopes. Here, Mike had an office with a door that said "The Bossman" in stick-on plastic letters. I looked around. The place was deserted.

If Mike was here, he was behind that door.

I hesitated, deflated and intimidated by my surroundings. But I wasn't there to let Darlene down. I stepped forward.

"Anybody home?" I called into the Bossman's partially opened doorway. When there was no answer, I pushed the door wide open. I walked into the room. I stopped.

There, in enemy territory, was one of our signs. It had been tossed onto the dirty carpet, next to Mighty Mike himself, who lay flat on his back, his head inside the knee space under his desk. What had I interrupted? What was Mike doing under his desk? Taking a nap? Fixing a drawer? Looking for gum?

I raised my voice and tried again.

"Mike, it's Valerie Rankin. As Darlene Mowat's campaign manager, I'm here to tell you to back off. Enough of your dirty tricks."

I waited. Mike didn't respond. I continued.

"It's all over social media. Pictures of dogs urinating on our signs. I know you're behind it. #barkformike? Really? What do you have to say for yourself?"

Apparently, nothing.

I picked up the sign. One of the girls had put good time into making it, and it would be a sin to waste all that work. As I reached down, I peered under the desk. I wasn't leaving until Mike talked to me.

That wasn't going to happen.

I didn't like the color of Mike's face. I liked the tight twist of the striped tie around his neck even less. I stood up. It was clear to me that Mighty Mike Murphy, long-time kingpin of Eastern Shore politics, was, for once, speechless.

He was dead.

With the sign still in my hand, I backed out of the room. What was I supposed to do now? Anyone, even a part-time sewing teacher and a full-time general store manager, could figure out that the man under the desk hadn't died without help. No one tied their own necktie that tight. Someone had killed Mike Murphy.

On purpose.

I had another thought.

A bad one.

If there was a victim in the building, maybe there was a killer here, too. I scanned the large room. I surveyed the piles of T-shirts, stacks of voter lists, and garbage bins overflowing with fast-food wrappers. Anyone could be hiding anywhere.

I had to get out.

Fast.

Holding Darlene's sign across my chest like a protective shield, I rushed to the main door. Out on the sidewalk, I ran past the windows covered with posters of Mike in happier, more animated times, to the safety of the Foodmart next door.

The minute my feet were through the automatic doors, I dumped the sign into a shopping cart. Fighting the resistance of four wheels going in different directions, I pushed the cart over to the first person I saw, the cashier at the 1–20 items-only checkout. Her name tag said "Mona." She saw the look on my face. She stopped smiling.

"Help! Call the police!" I shouted. Mona stepped back. She banged her hip on the bag hook.

"The Mounties? Why? Lock yourself out of your car?" she asked. Lots of people did that, no need to panic, her face said.

"No, no," I shrieked. "It's Mike. The mayor. Next door at his headquarters. He's dead. I think he's been murdered."

For a fraction of a second, Mona was still.

Then, she transformed.

Right in front of my eyes, the cashier changed from a supermarket employee into a rise-to-the-occasion local woman, ready to handle any crisis life sent her way. In one smooth movement, Mona grabbed the phone next to her cash register and reached across the rubber conveyor belt to squeeze my hand in hers.

I heard her voice above us, over the loudspeaker. "Manager to cash nine, manager to cash nine. On the double." She hung up the phone and tore off her Foodmart apron. "Don't worry my dear. The manager will call the RCMP. We're going to the lunchroom. You and I need a cup of tea."

Later, as Mona and I sat with our cups under a row of coats, I remembered the sign in the cart.

How stupid was I? I'd been at the scene of a crime.

And what had I done? Walked straight out with evidence in my hand.

This was not good.

It looked suspicious. The first thing the Royal Canadian Mounted Police would wonder, when they found Mike strangled under a desk, was who did it.

And if I were the RCMP, who would I talk to first?

Me.

CHAPTER THREE

I missed the arrival of the ambulance, two reporters, and the crowd of local people who arrived after Mona made her calls. I wasn't outside—I was in an RCMP cruiser.

Were they going to arrest me?

To keep my mind off this possibility, I tried to make conversation. I knew the officer at the wheel. Dawn Nolan and I had done police business before. I also knew that she rented Sylvie's basement apartment. Sylvie said that she was nice. Quiet, but nice. I counted on that now.

"It was quite the shock," I said. "Finding Mike under the desk like that. Dead."

"I can imagine," Officer Nolan said, glancing over at me. "Are you alright?"

"As good as can be expected. I was there because of the dogs," I explained. "There's nothing wrong with liking cats, you know. It doesn't mean you don't like dogs." I paused and looked at Officer Nolan. She was concentrating on her driving.

The RCMP officer was careful in her reply. "Right. For now, all we need are the facts. You understand?"

I wasn't sure. I didn't know anything about Mike's death, but if the RCMP wanted to be formal, that was fine with me.

"I was there in the office, being a campaign manager," I continued. Why did I never know when to stop talking? "Darlene and I read that booklet, you know, *A Guide for Women Running in Elections*? It's nine pages, covers everything, but it skips dirty tricks. That's why I went to see Mike. Those dogs are ruining our signs."

Officer Nolan kept her eyes on the road.

When we arrived at the station, Dawn Nolan left me in a room that, for various reasons, I had been in before. After a wait of about thirty minutes, she and her senior officer, Wade Corkum, walked in.

Everyone knew Wade. He was one of those former high school star athletes who secretly spend their lives wondering whether Grade 12 had been the best year of their lives. In Wade's case, the yearning to belong and wear a uniform had led him to the RCMP. As a Mountie, he was moderately successful. He counted on the sparse population to keep him no busier than he wanted to be. I often saw him lounging in his cruiser along the highway, his speed gun steady on the dashboard.

Today, Wade was flustered. Before he sat down, he took off his RCMP hat and threw it on the table. The elaborate crest, *Maintiens le droit*, meaning "uphold the right," spun and then settled to face me. Under the overhead lights, Wade's shaved head glowed. I thought that I could see the joints of the tectonic plates of his skull. I caught myself staring. Wade cleared his throat.

"Looks like you had yourself had quite the morning," he said, then turned formal. "Officer Nolan will record this interview. We'll transcribe it. You'll sign it for accuracy. Are you comfortable with the process?"

Wade's politeness worried me. I knew that he found me irritating. Something was up.

But who says no to the Mounties?

"Sure," I said. "Mike was dead when I found him. I hope you don't think that I had anything to do with it." There was no response. I tried to think of something else to say.

"I'm a mother," I offered. This should make clear that I was not capable of murder. Granted, my three children were now adults, at least in their own minds. And yes, they lived far away from Gasper's Cove. That was beside the point. I was a mother, a sewing teacher, and a crafter. I was *not* someone who killed mayors. I had nothing else to say. I wanted to go home. I wanted to see my dog.

Wade sighed. I felt better. An annoyed Wade was more familiar.

"Look. You're here for a statement. Then, we will wait for the results from the medical examiner. Let's stick to that for now," he said.

"I'm not a suspect?" I asked. I wanted to make sure.

"We will be thorough," Wade said, evading my question. He glanced at Nolan, indicating that thoroughness would be her job. "But on the face of it, violence, moving a body under a desk, and laying a competitor's sign beside the victim don't strike me as your *modus operandi*."

"Modus what?" I asked. The term had a familiar, heard-on-TV sound to it.

Wade almost let himself smile.

"The way you do things," he explained. "You are more of a missing-sewing-machine, busybody, not-able-to-mind-your-own-business kind of operator. More likely to get in the way of trouble than to make it. At least, that's how it's been up to now."

Nolan leaned forward, ready to get back to business.

"Let's begin with what you know about the former mayor," she said. "What did you think of him?"

I put my purse on the table and took off my red boiled-wool jacket. I folded it over the back of the chair and settled in. Where should I start?

Nolan was new in town. There was a lot she wouldn't know. "He was a fight promoter before he went into politics," I told her. "That's where he got his nickname, 'Mighty Mike.' Skinny little guy, managing a bunch of bruisers from the woods or off the boats. His boxers called him that."

Wade interrupted. "Small-time fights," he explained to Nolan. "Mike drove around the province, charging for brawls that were going to happen anyway. You know, on Friday nights, paydays."

I nodded. Wade grew up here, so he knew. None of Mike's boxers lasted long. Most had more belligerence than skill. Or mothers who made them quit fighting.

"What made him move from that to the mayor's office?" Nolan asked.

"Fight promotion is hand to mouth. I figure he wanted a better job. Besides, he could use the same skill set," I answered. We all saw it. Boxing had taught Mike to talk fast, exaggerate his achievements, and pass over money in a handshake. It also taught him that everything in life was a fight. "I think what Mike liked most about being mayor was getting there," I said. "He liked elections. Always a clear winner and a loser."

Dawn Nolan made a note and passed it over to Wade. They both looked at me.

"Just to be clear," Nolan said, "in your opinion, Mayor Murphy had enough"—she searched for the right word—"*conflict* in his past that someone might have held a grudge against him, is that right?"

Wade took over. "Anyone you can think of?" he asked.

"Not really," I said. "But I've heard Mike would bend the rules in return for a little compensation. Who knows what he was up to?" I rubbed my index finger and thumb together like I had seen them do in the movies, vaguely aware that I was getting carried away. "Then, there's the election. Fewer people running, the better his chances." As soon as the words had left my mouth, I realized that wasn't a smart thing to say. Not for myself, and not for Darlene. "But you can count Darlene out. She's my cousin, on my mother's side."

Wade picked up his hat. "I think we have all we need from you," he sighed. "More than we need, in fact. You are free to go today. We know where to find you." The corners of his mouth twitched. "Can't say you're much of a flight risk."

"Flight risk?" I was grateful for TV. It was helping me interpret this conversation. "You mean, leave Gasper's Cove? Where else would I go?"

"Exactly," Wade said opening the door for me. "We'll talk again soon. Count on it."

⟳

I was beat, but when I returned home, Toby's big golden retriever face was at the window. How long he had been there on the couch, paws on the African violets on the windowsill, waiting? I was late for his walk. Not surprisingly, as soon as my foot touched the first step, I heard the rattle of his harness and leash as they were dragged to the front entry. So, as tired as I was, off we went.

We were halfway down the street when my phone beeped in my pocket. The call was from Darlene's director of communications, Sarah Chisholm. Sarah was her own kind of verbal news station. I suspected her reach, at least locally, was wider and deeper than that of the Canadian Broadcasting Corporation. She'd been the obvious choice to handle media relations for the campaign.

"Have you heard?" she demanded.

"Not only heard it—I was there. Poor Mike," I said. I assumed that we were talking about the mayor's murder.

"Mike? Oh, yes. He's dead. But that's not it. Look at the *Lighthouse Online*."

"Hang on, hang on," I said, "give me a minute." I tapped away. In seconds, I had the latest edition on my screen. "What am I looking for?"

"Read the headline. Do you believe this?" Sarah sounded energized.

"Okay," I said, scrolling.

"'License no longer required for dip-netting Gaspereau'?" My fishermen uncles would be pleased.

"Nope, keep reading," she coached.

"'Stabbed Halifax man taken to hospital returned home to stab stabber. Both recovering'?" Another reason I was happy I had left the big city. It said that they were roommates.

"'Two forged paintings found hanging in the premier's office'?" Fakes in Province House? No surprise there.

"'Man breaks into Tim Horton's to make himself a coffee'?" I continued. I had felt like doing that myself on occasion.

"Keep going." Sarah was impatient.

"'Beer bottle as old as Canada found floating on local beach'?" Probably left behind by the stabbing roommates.

"No, no, no," she said. "Look at the bottom. Regional news."

I saw it.

There it was.

"'Long-time mayor of Drummond found dead at campaign office by a middle-aged passerby.'"

"'Passerby'?" I choked. "I wasn't passing by, I went there for a reason. To ream the guy out for his smear campaign against us. It was dog exploitation!"

"Looks like someone there before you did a better reaming-out job. Keep going, the best one is farther down," Sarah said.

I was still offended. "'Middle-aged'? Not even close. I'm definitely on the right side of fifty."

"Let it go. Read," Sarah ordered.

"'Election Launch to go on as planned on the Drummond Waterfront tomorrow.' I don't believe it," I said. They were going to carry on as if a murder hadn't happened? "Is that in good taste?"

"Of course not," Sarah said. "That's the point. Look at the story."

I did.

"It's what Mighty Mike would have wanted. For democracy to continue," says former deputy mayor Elliot Carter.

"My heart is heavy, but I know that the best way to

honor Mike's legacy is to continue it. That's the reason
I'm entering the race myself. This one's for Mike."

The report went on.

With the death of the former mayor, four candidates remain
in the race. In addition to former deputy mayor Carter, also
director of the Gasper's Cove Public Works Department, the
candidates are Charlie Landry, a well-known local activist,
who has run in the last nine elections; Brian Nickerson, lawyer,
businessman, and president of the St. Francis Xavier University
Alumni Association; and Darlene Mowat, a vocal opponent
of amalgamation. A local hair stylist, Mowat is the three-time
winner of the Nova Scotia provincial updo competition.

May the most-qualified candidate win.

"What do you think?" Sarah asked, so loudly that I had to
move the phone away from my ear.

"What I think are two things," I said. "First, we've got to
keep Darlene strong." There was only one way to do that.
"I'm making her a new outfit."

"What's the other thing?" Sarah asked.

"We're putting Darlene on the waterfront tomorrow with
people who are out to get her." I paused. "And one of them is
a killer."

CHAPTER FOUR

Dressing Darlene for political battle was a challenge.

Darlene had the misfortune to become a DD cup size in Grade 6. This gotten her a lot of attention. It had also brought her heartbreak and three failed marriages. But you had to give Darlene credit—when the last husband had run out on Christmas Eve, taking the new rubber floor mats and the windshield ice scraper, Darlene had pulled herself up by her acrylic nails. She'd gone down to the basement and set up her salon. She'd run for town council and won. And now she was running for mayor. Becoming her campaign manager was the least I could do. But it wasn't an easy job. Not when it meant that I had to tell her what to wear.

"Black?! You're kidding." Darlene was indignant. "You might as well say beige." She hitched up the cross-over portion of her floral polyester dress. "You know my colors: coral, shocking pink, turquoise, and periwinkle. How about I do the launch in my periwinkle palazzo pants and matching shell? With coral accessories and shoes? What do you think?"

I considered this ensemble, her favorite, worn to the last Chamber of Commerce dinner and dance. The shell had sequins on it. I visualized tomorrow's podium on the waterfront. I saw a row of men in gabardine. I saw Darlene in an outfit that swirled when she step-danced.

"How about a suit?" I suggested. "A dark blue suit."

"What?" Darlene rolled her eyes. "I'm running for mayor, not enlisting in the navy."

This wasn't going to be easy. But I remembered the article in the *Lighthouse*. I couldn't give up.

"How about a dress?" I tried. "I have some fabric at home." I couldn't say that it was brown—that would turn her right off. "Deep ... mocha. Perfect for the coral shoes and jewelry."

Darlene relented. "Okay, but make it fitted. And don't go to any trouble."

"I won't," I lied. "I'll whip it up after dinner."

It took me three hours, but before I went to bed, the dress was done. It was a simple ponte sheath sewn on the serger, with a catch-stitched hem. If I'd had more time, I would have made her a proper coat dress. Under pressure, the fastest thing to make was a knit. I'd read that brown was the color of reliability. Given that this dress was for Darlene, and for her first public event in the campaign, I thought that deep mocha wouldn't hurt.

Before the causeway was built more than 30 years ago, the communities of Gasper's Cove and Drummond were connected by a ferry that ran twice a day. When the ferry was no longer needed, it was retired to the Drummond side. There, it was moored next to an apron of asphalt called the

"Historical Interpretive Centre," optimistically intended, along with the small building behind it, to be a tourist attraction. Staging the launch in front of the old ferry was supposed to express a connection between the two communities. This purpose was lost when the small podium was set up in the parking lot with its back to Gasper's Cove across the water. Facing the podium was a semicircle of folding chairs with a small riser for TV cameras behind them. By the time Darlene and I arrived, the camera people were already there, as were as a few reporters, one of whom I knew, Noah Dixon. Noah was a surfing friend of my youngest son, Paul. I knew that Noah did some reporting for the CBC in Halifax but had recently become a staff writer for the *Lighthouse*.

I made a beeline for him as soon we arrived.

"Noah," I called out. "Tell me that you had nothing to do with 'Catty Candidate Disses Dogs.'"

"Oh, that. Not me," he said, reaching up to loosen the collar of the button-down shirt he had put on for the event. "I wanted to cover more of the election, but they're moving me to sports."

"It was a cheap shot, whoever wrote it," I said, moving to let a cameraman with heavy gear go past. "I'm surprised to see so much media here today."

"Are you kidding?" Noah asked. "This is a big story. Outgoing mayor killed, crime unsolved at the start of an election? Might even go national. A real career opportunity for whoever covers it."

A clipboard jabbed my back. It belonged to the event organizer.

"I'd like to stay on schedule," she said, making a show of looking at her watch. "Could you please have Miss Mowat wait in the interpretive center with the other candidates? I'd like to march them all out together when we start."

I mumbled something that I hoped she would think was an apology. I said goodbye to Noah and went to find Darlene, who had wandered off. As I pushed through the crowd, I passed Trevor Ross, a local teacher. Trevor's hair was falling out of his ponytail as he tried to control his class from the junior high.

"Hi Trevor," I said. "I thought you taught art. What are you doing here?"

"Pulled the short straw," he said. "The principal thought that they should see democracy in action. I was the one with the free period." He looked past me over my shoulder, and his eyes widened. "Hey, boys! Get away from the water!" he shouted, then turned to me. "Nice to see you, got to go."

The clipboard hit my back again. I found Darlene, took her by the arm, and we hurried up the stairs to the center. At the doors, she hesitated.

"What's wrong?" I asked as I pushed her inside. "You look agitated. Nerves?"

Darlene lifted up her bright statement necklace. "No, it's this," she said, showing me a faint red rash on her neck.

I leaned in and caught a whiff of Darlene's L'Air du Temps. "It's probably nothing. Don't worry about it," I said, distracted. Around us, I saw the other campaign managers with their candidates, rehearsing speeches, prepping for Q&As. We weren't doing any of that. I had been preoccupied with clothing, not with content.

"Darlene, we should have done our homework," I whispered.

"Don't stress about it. I know what to say," she said, arranging her necklace to cover the rash. "Calm down."

I willed myself to relax. Then, I saw an unexpected face on the far side of the room.

Stuart Campbell.

Stuart was a local engineer I had met when we renovated the store's second floor for the Co-op. He was a single dad and the father of Erin, one of our junior crafters. Once or twice in the past, Stuart and I had almost had a moment. If you asked me, as Darlene often did, about the status of our relationship, I would say that he was someone I would be interested in, if I were interested in being interested. Which I was not. I wasn't sure whether this response was true, but it felt safe. I had a busy life. Where was the time for romance?

Despite this stance, I felt a lift when I saw Stuart's blue eyes and dark hair across the room. That lift fell when I saw that he was with Brian Nickerson, candidate for mayor. I marched across the room, grabbed Stuart's arm, and pulled him aside.

"What are you doing here? With that guy?" I asked under my breath. Brian was a few steps away, giving some local power broker the two-armed shake, one hand in the man's palm, the other squeezing the man's bicep. His father, Senator Bryce Nickerson, stood next to him, beaming as he watched his son execute the move as instructed.

"What does it look like? I'm Brian's campaign manager," Stuart whispered back. "We go way back. College roommates," he added, as if this fact explained everything. "How about you?"

"I'm running Darlene's campaign," I said with authority. The only roommates Darlene and I had in our past were siblings in bunk beds. "She's the smartest person I know."

"I hope so," Stuart said. "It's crazy what she's doing. You know that, don't you?" He turned his back to Brian to talk to me. "I'd hate to see her waste her time. Brian is convinced that small independent communities can't make it on their own."

And whose reality is that? I thought, studying the campaign button on Stuart's lapel: *Nickerson for Progress. Prosperity. Purpose.*

"What does that even mean?" I asked, nodding at the badge. "Sounds corporate. Who came up with that cheesy slogan?"

"Me," Stuart said. He pointed to the badge on my sweater. "You make those yourself? Cute."

I reached down and angled the pin upward so I could see it. Our team had cross-stitched them while they watched reruns of *Downton Abbey*.

"We did," I said. "We're originals."

Stuart and I looked at each other in silence. I wanted him to say that this was all silly, that none of it mattered. He didn't. Too late, I realized that those could have, should have, been my words.

A bell rang. The group of candidates moved toward the door.

"See you outside," I whispered.

Stuart smiled and moved away.

$$\sim \! 0 \! \sim$$

This election launch was the first I had attended. As a result, being apolitical and involved only because of a relative, I didn't have much to judge it against. However, I thought that things went well, at least until the end.

It started with Elliot Carter pushing his way to the microphone before anyone else had a chance. There, he intoned long and hard about how his heavy heart left him no choice but to run for mayor. He said, "This one's for Mike" at least forty-seven times. Bored, I watched and wondered whether Elliot had any blood in him. Everything about the man was narrow and pale: a long nose; gray hair cut in what used to be called a brush cut; the legs of his pants, lapels, and tie, all narrow. He reminded me of a snake, or at least someone who would slide into a room sideways. I wouldn't have voted for him.

Charlie Landry, bless him, was next. Charlie looked like he did every time he ran for office: His long beard was moderately twig-free; his rubber sandals were strapped tightly over thick, pilled cotton socks; his green corduroy pants were too short; and his mis-buttoned pink shirt was too long. He began by mentioning the deceased mayor but didn't have the sense to stop there. Instead, he went on to imply that Mike's death was connected to the former mayor's position on the nesting areas of the piping plover, as if a gang of birds had invaded Mike's office and tightened that tie. Only the students applauded when he finished.

Brian Nickerson was up next. He smiled at his father and then asked for a minute of silence in Mike's honor, offering the family his thoughts and prayers. He followed this moment by explaining that the town of Drummond had never been well run, presumably a different sort of reference to Mike, and promised that, if elected, which he appeared to expect, he would do things differently. These changes would involve dragging our communities into this century, securing outside investment, and cutting fat so the newly combined Gasper's Cove/Drummond would run like a well-oiled machine.

The attendees stirred in their seats and waited for Darlene to speak. She, they knew, would at least be unpredictable.

Darlene got right to it.

"With all due respect to the last speaker, who wants to live in a machine?" she asked. A few of the older people chuckled. "What we need around here is someone who remembers who we are. The first thing I will do when I'm mayor is hold a public vote on this amalgamation thing." She paused and looked directly into the cameras pointed at her. "But that's not all. Another face should have been here today and isn't. I am not even sure whether it's respectful for the rest of us to have this event. A terrible thing happened in this community. A man was murdered. That shouldn't happen anywhere, and it sure as heck shouldn't happen on the eastern shore of Nova Scotia. It hurts our hearts. As a result, election or no election, I'm going to do everything I can to get to the bottom of what happened to Mike. Then, we can discuss other things. I promise."

The crowd applauded—that is, nearly everyone did. During Darlene's speech, I felt two people come and stand quietly beside me.

When the clapping stopped, Officers Wade Corkum and Dawn Nolan moved forward. They walked up to the podium.

"Glad to hear that, Miss Mowat," Wade said. "But I am going to ask you to come with us. We would like to question you in reference to the murder of Michael Murphy."

The cameras kept rolling. Noah started taking notes.

CHAPTER FIVE

I didn't hear from Darlene all that evening.

What did this silence mean? Were they fingerprinting her and taking mugshots? Had she asked them to photograph her best side? How much trouble was she in? In my life, I dealt with uncertainty with action. But what action could I take now? I couldn't exactly phone up the RCMP and ask, "Are you done with my cousin yet?"

I had to wait.

I'm no good at waiting, never have been. So, when there wasn't any word the next morning, there was only one thing to do. It was time to consult a larger force. Toby and I needed the ocean.

Together, we drove to the top part of the island and the rocky beaches. On the way, we passed the yacht club, and near it, the bend to the Bluenose Inn. On impulse, I decided to stop at the inn. It belonged to my cousin Rollie and the town's former librarian, Catherine Walker.

Rollie was wise. He would say what I needed to hear.

I had to admit, I was surprised when Rollie and Catherine bought the old bed-and-breakfast. Being an innkeeper was my cousin's third career. After all, he was a trained psychologist, one who had been in private practice and worked in the provincial prison system. He was good at his profession, and the family was proud of him, one of the few who'd gone to university. However, when my aunt Dot, who had been managing the general store, moved south and the family needed someone to run the business, Rollie had stepped up. He was the kind of man who always did.

Rollie's second career didn't go as smoothly as his first. He tried hard to be a store manager, but because he was born to listen, not to sell, the role wore on him. Despite this, when he announced that he was leaving the store, I was shocked. I had drawn up a plan for my empty-nest future and penciled Rollie into it. I had assumed that the family was all either of us needed. But then, right under my oblivious nose, Rollie had fallen in love.

$$\infty$$

Rollie and Catherine had owned the inn for six months. They hoped to be open for guests by summer. Getting there was more work than they had expected. The previous owners hadn't redecorated since 1984. As a result, Rollie and Catherine had to gut much of the inn's interior. A giant rental dumpster was installed in the yard, and it was soon filled with dusty rose wallpaper, threadbare towels, musty shag carpet, and lumpy comforters well past use, all thrown out of the upstairs windows.

Today, when I approached the inn, I could see that the dumpster was gone. In its place, the lawn had been trimmed up to the edge of the cliff overlooking the ocean. I was impressed—that is, until I saw the sign hammered into the ground next to the one for the inn itself:

Brian for Progress. Prosperity. Purpose.

I couldn't believe it.

My cousin. What was he thinking? I parked my car on the horseshoe driveway and, taking Toby with me for support, stormed into the old building. I found Rollie and Catherine in the dining room.

"What's going on?" I asked them from the doorway. "Why do you have a sign for Brian Nickerson out there? What about Darlene? Have you forgotten that we have a member of this family running for mayor?"

Catherine looked at me calmly. She laid a pen and a tiny packet of yellow sticky notes down on the lace tablecloth. I saw that she was cataloging the serving dishes. As I came closer, I could read the labels, written in thick black marker: "Breakfast, eggs"; "Luncheon, finger sandwiches"; "Teatime, petits fours." On the table was a diagram with dish dimensions, showing where each item was to be stored.

"Strictly speaking, Darlene is *your* cousin, not Rollie's," she said. "She's on your mother's side, not your dad's. You are the point of connection, not us."

Toby moved closer to me and put a paw over my foot. *Don't do it*, he telegraphed. *Don't say anything you'll regret. Deep breath, take a deep breath.* Then, like a yoga teacher coaching a class, he yawned and let out a swoosh of air.

He was right. But this situation was hard.

"That has nothing to do with anything," I said. Who was this woman to talk about our family with an *us*? "That sign is a betrayal. You know what everyone will think, don't you? Why should they vote for Darlene when her own relatives won't?"

Rollie stepped down from a small ladder. He had been sent up to retrieve even more dishes from the top of a massive walnut china cabinet. He carefully placed three huge, heavy platters on the dining room table and dusted his hands on a floral apron.

"It's not about betraying anyone," he said. "We simply looked at each campaign's policies and platform"—he hesitated, aware that what he was about to say next would set me off—"and relevant experience and background."

Catherine nodded like a bobblehead doll. "Being part of a larger municipality makes sense. Brian has promised to increase taxes on people renting out rooms privately. That would mean a lot to innkeepers like us. He'll meet the challenges of the times."

This talk all sounded like something Catherine had read in a brochure. I looked at the dishes on the table. I looked at the hands that had arranged them.

Then, I got it.

The real reason for the sign out front.

Both Rollie and Catherine had *the ring* on their right hands. Big square gold rings with large black Xs on them—no words, just an X. The St. Francis Xavier University ring, known country-wide across the seats of power as "the X-Ring." My dad used to call it the secret decoder ring of Canadian politics. Wearers of the ring, earned in a small, historic university in rural Nova Scotia, were enormously and disproportionally represented in Canadian politics and government. The current resident of the premier's office in Halifax wore one, as did half his deputy ministers. St. Xavier's undergraduate enrollment of only 3,000 annually produced graduates who ran the country, from the prime minister's office, from the House of Commons, and from provincial Houses of Assemblies, coast to coast.

The secret society was at work. Again.

"I don't believe it," I said. I was disappointed with Rollie *and* with our town's former librarian. "You all went to the same university. That's it, isn't it?" I knew that I sounded shrill, but I didn't care. "So, you've had a few glasses of chardonnay with this guy in some faculty lounge. That doesn't mean the senator's son knows what he's doing." Toby sighed, lay down on the worn carpet, and stared at the wall. He knew when to give up.

"It's not like that," Catherine said, trying and failing to placate me. "We respect Darlene. Maybe she should run for council again, not for mayor. And with the Mounties taking her in for questioning ... you must admit, it's a distraction."

"Distraction from what? That thing with the RCMP is going to get cleared up real soon. You can bet on it. But what is she supposed to do? Go back to the sidelines where she belongs?" I was working myself up to full emotional speed. "Why don't you say it? Darlene is just a hairdresser, a three-time divorcée, and a one-term, small-town councillor from an island off the coast of nowhere. Her life's too messy for you, isn't it?" I paused for breath.

Catherine and Rollie exchanged an uneasy look.

"But everyone's life is messy," I continued. "Life's no alumni association cocktail party. When it's messy, you want someone who knows how it feels, who knows how to get back up. That's Darlene. Don't talk to me about '*relevant* experience.'"

Having run out of words, but not out of rage, I moved to the door. Toby got up and followed me, as eager as I was to find some fresh air. Catherine and Rollie didn't move. Instead, they sat at the big oval table in silence, surrounded by someone else's past, which they now hoped to renovate into a future for themselves.

Progress.

I looked down at the large dishes and the tiny yellow sticky notes.

"Those platters," I said, pointing to the dishes Rollie had put down, "are chipped. Get rid of them. Some of this stuff is getting old. Real old."

CHAPTER SIX

After I loaded Toby into the car and buckled my seat belt, I looked at my hands on the steering wheel. It had been a long time since a wedding ring had been on my left hand. But on my right, there was a ring. One Darlene and I had bought ourselves when we turned twenty-one. A silver claddagh ring, two hands holding a heart underneath a crown. It represented friendship, love, and loyalty.

I looked at the treacherous sign in front of the inn, picked up my phone, and texted Sarah.

Do me a favor?

Sure.

You have the email list. Can you contact the crafters?

Yes.

A meeting tonight. After supper. My place.

Okay. Why?

Darlene needs us.

Got it.

I felt better. I turned my key in the ignition, but the car was slow to catch. Great, just what I needed, a repair bill. My phone beeped on the seat beside me. I allowed myself a moment of self-pity and then picked it up.

Noah.

Normally, I liked talking to Noah. He was the same age as my sons. His voice made me feel that they were not so far away. Now, I was wary of talking to a reporter. Words, I was learning, could hurt. But I was Darlene's manager. I pressed *Accept call.*

"This better not be 'Catty Candidate Caught,'" I said. "Darlene's helping the RCMP with their inquiries. She's not arrested." *At least not yet,* I thought.

"Don't worry, not covering that one. I have something else for you. I owe you," Noah said. "Something that might make you feel better."

"I could sure use that. What do you have?"

"Okay. Two stories. This is the first one. The country-wide crime stats are out. Get this: We have the highest per-capita rate of crimes *solved* of any community in Canada. We are more likely to report crimes and more likely to solve them. It's a big story." I caught the excitement in Noah's voice. Another great opportunity for his big break.

But this statistic confused me. "I don't get it," I said. "There has to be more crime in the big cities, and they have more police on the job."

"That's the thing, isn't it?" Noah agreed. "In a larger center, if they find a guy in a snowbank or at the bottom of the stairs, they call it an accident. But here, people talk; they get involved. There's a prof at St. Francis Xavier who wrote a paper on it." I heard rustling in the background. "I have it right here. The title is hilarious. Do you want to hear it?"

"Sure."

"The Effect of Informal Fact-Finding Processes in Rural Communities as a Multifaceted Agent in the Resolution of Criminal Events," Noah read.

"Excuse me?"

"This professor guy has a name for it: 'productive gossip.'" Noah laughed. "He thinks we're experts. No one here gets away with anything because we're nosey."

I leaned back in the car seat to consider this. Last winter, I dropped a hand-knitted red mitten in the middle of Front Street. By the time I got home, two people had called, one to tell me that she'd rescued it from the slush, and the other to ask whether she could borrow the pattern.

"Maybe the professor has a point," I said, finally. "What's the other story? You said there were two."

"Best for last," Noah said. "It looks like the RCMP wants to prove that their rural force is as good as the city's. They loved these new statistics. They're sending a bigwig down from Ottawa to present an award to Wade Corkum, for having the highest solve-to-crime ratio in the country. I interviewed him about it."

Wade? An award for police excellence? For once, I was almost speechless. "How's he taking it?"

"It took about 40 seconds for the idea he was a crack investigator to go to his head," Noah said. "He's all jacked up. Desperate to demonstrate his expertise before the brass arrives. I figure that's why he went after Darlene at a public event. He's showing off."

Knowing Wade, this made sense. He hadn't won a thing since high school.

"Just what we need," I said. "An arrest-happy RCMP officer. Thanks for letting me know."

"No problem," Noah said. "Watch for the story."

⌒𝄐⌒

By seven o'clock that evening, twenty of Darlene's friends and supporters were in my living room. Tilly Ferguson had even brought her granddaughter Megan, and Megan's friend Emma, a nice girl from the city. In no time, the coffee table was covered with plates of cranberry loaf, oatcakes, molasses cookies, scones, and blueberry muffins. It looked like the spread at a wake. In a sense, it was. What had started as a craft-supported run for mayor had ended up with the candidate in jail. As Emma helped me refill the teacups, I explained why Darlene was still with the Mounties.

"It's something called 'investigative detention.' Dawn Nolan explained it to me," I said. "If they think that you know something about a crime, including that you did it yourself, they can hold you until you tell them everything." I raised my hand as the women in the living room objected. "It was the sign that did it," I said. "The one that was next to Mike."

"You're joking." Sarah looked up from her phone. "Because it was her name was on the sign? That doesn't mean that she killed him."

"It's not that simple," I said. "I guess Darlene's fingerprints were on the sign, and red hair was on his jacket. Wade's building a case."

"Oh, come on now," Annette said. "Darlene's been on the causeway, waving at cars all week. Everyone has seen her. That's where the fingerprints came from, and probably the hair too."

"Let's hope that Wade figures that out," I said. "We'll have to wait and see. They took a sample, you know, for evidence."

"Do you mean of her hair?" Sylvie asked, putting down her crochet, her latest obsession. Tonight, she was wearing a pullover inspired by the Maud Lewis painting *Three Black Cats*. The mother and her two kittens looked content against the green background and a row of bright tulips. A tourist had tried to buy the sweater. Sylvie had said no, it was an original.

"Yes, the red hair," I said. "Wade thinks it's Darlene's. When the lab confirms it, he might arrest her."

"Poor Darlene. How was she when they took her in?" Annette asked. I'd followed the cruiser to the RCMP detachment and had a minute with my cousin before she was led away.

"Calm but chatty," I said. "All she said was to feed the cats and clean the litter boxes."

Sarah lifted her face from her phone. "Maybe this isn't as bad as we think," she told the group. "As long as Darlene doesn't end up spending the rest of her life in prison, she might do okay in the election. Look at these polls." She held up her phone so we could see the tiny graph on the screen. "Her poll numbers are better than they were before the launch. If we can get the RCMP to hold her all week, we might even win this thing."

"That would be good, I guess," Tilly muttered. "But in the meantime, what are we supposed to do?"

"I've got a to-do list," I said, pulling it out of my pocket. "Darlene had it in her purse and gave it to me." I cleared my throat and read:

1. Signs on more lawns. Tell voters that they are the same as the one found next to Mike. Collector's items?

2. Order Mac Studio Fix liquid foundation (N6.5, medium peachy beige). Might be the only good coverage I get.

3. Tell Charlie Landry not to chant "Free all political prisoners" in front of the station if I am arrested.

4. Knock on doors. Everybody does it.

I put down the list. Annette got to her feet and headed to the basement stairs.

"Where are you going?" I called after her.

"I'm going to get more of those signs stenciled up," she said. "After the dogs, we need them."

"Hang on, get back here. We need to talk canvassing," I told her. Annette returned to the living room and sat down.

"Does anyone know anything about door-knocking?" I asked.

"Mike was the expert—it was the only reason he was elected," Sarah said, her thumb scrolling on her phone. "Look at this." She held up the screen again, and we saw a picture of Mike in better days, holding his shoe up for the camera.

I leaned in. "What on Earth is he doing?"

"What he did at the start of every election," Sarah said. "He would put a piece of cardboard inside each of his shoes. He made a big deal about how he wore it out walking, meeting the voters."

"Such a nuisance," Tilly said. "If you opened the door, that man would come right in the house. Always found something 'in common' to talk about, mostly made up. Know what I mean?"

Three women on the couch, all neighbors, nodded.

"He saw a picture on the mantle of my dad in his uniform. Told me his father was in the navy," said one.

The woman next to her looked surprised. "Navy? He told me that his dad worked in the shipyards. Same as mine."

"The uncle." The crafter at the end of the couch laughed. "Did he tell you about his uncle? The one who invented Morse code? Worked with Marconi?"

Sylvie leaned forward. "He tried to convince me the picture on this sweater was done by a kid at the school," she said, rolling her eyes. "He said no real artist painted like that."

"I've got a better one," Annette chimed in. "You know when my parents went to Cuba? He said he would hand-deliver the passport forms to the house, for a small fee."

"Are you kidding me?" I asked. "They have stacks at the post office for free."

"My point exactly," Annette said, reaching for another oatcake. "The man was a crook, but he knew how to win elections. Cardboard in his shoes. I guess that's what it takes."

Canvassing? Going door-to-door? I cringed. Darlene thought that it was important, but did we have to do it?

How would we start? I had no idea.

But I knew who to ask.

CHAPTER SEVEN

Charlie Landry and I met at the Agapi restaurant. I ordered baklava and tea. Charlie had a short black and an apple from his pocket.

"You want to know how to canvass," Charlie said. "Good thing. Going right to the people, hearing their concerns." He paused to sip from the tiny cup, his pinky delicately extended like some grandfather attending a granddaughter's tea party. "Of course, some people close the door on you or pretend they're not home. Old Mike was a master. If no one came to the door, he'd go around back, look in the windows, tap on the glass. His persistence got him elected, nothing else."

"But how do *we* get started?" I asked. "I really appreciate the benefit of your experience, particularly because you're running for mayor too."

Charlie put his doll's cup down and wiped his beard with a paper napkin. "It's the democratic process I'm interested in, not winning," he said. For the first time, I noticed the ring on his finger. Gold, no words, just the letter X. "Besides,

Darlene is running against the Brian and Elliot patriarchy. We're in that fight together. Detention down at police headquarters was to be expected."

The patriarchy? I couldn't resist. "I didn't know you went to St. Francis Xavier," I said, gesturing to his hand.

Charlie laughed. "Oh, yes. I grew up in Belmont, Massachusetts. I was a bit of a rabble-rouser back in the day. The family thought if they shipped me off to a nice little Jesuit college in Nova Scotia, I'd forget about politics." Charlie laughed so hard that the table shook. "I felt I'd found Brigadoon as soon as I got here. I belonged. When I finished my biology degree, I stayed. The family paid to keep me from coming home," he said with a wink. "Lucky me."

Aha, this explained a lot, I thought. No visible job, Charlie's name on every ballot, and his willingness to share his experience with a competitor. I was sitting across from an independently wealthy freethinker. And one who knew more about running in elections than I did.

"On the ground, what should we do?" I asked. "We've got to keep going once she's finished with the RCMP."

Charlie leaned forward with enthusiasm. "Rule one: Have an advance person. Someone who runs a few houses ahead and relays back intelligence before you get there. Things like a competitor's sign, large dogs on the premises, anything to help you read the street."

"What do you mean?"

"Well, if there are bikes on the sidewalk, make sure you talk about education. If the flower garden is weedless, discuss seniors' issues. Overalls on the clothesline, talk about problems in the fishery," Charlie smiled. He knew more than I had suspected. "Most elections I'm on my own, but this time, Kenny MacQuarrie, the president of the birders, is onboard. He supports my position on the piping plover and osprey nesting areas."

Charlie signaled to George Kosoulus that he needed another coffee. The pause gave me time to think. Did our campaign have a policy on birds? We should. The dog and cat issue had been explosive enough. We needed to make clear that we were for the nests too. I'd take care of it. But I had one more question to ask, and it wasn't politically related.

"You seem to know this stuff pretty well," I started. "I keep thinking about Mike. From your experience, who would want a municipal politician dead?"

Charlie looked me right in the eye and appeared to make some sort of calculation before he answered.

"No politician is who they seem. Remember that," he said, his voice quiet. "This game runs on ego and ambition. There's no way of knowing how much of that's in anybody or what it will make them do. It's the friendly ones you have to watch. Never underestimate anyone. Get what I'm saying?"

I wasn't sure that I did. I picked up the bill and thanked Charlie for his time. As I walked to the cash register, I looked back. Charlie was laying a pamphlet on the table like a tip, one he'd recycled for the current election by putting a sticker over the old date.

What would possibly motivate anyone to keep running for office, election after election, year after year, if all they ever did was lose? What drove a man like Charlie?

Maybe he had just told me.

Outside the doors of the restaurant, I almost ran into Stuart Cameron and Brian Nickerson. Both men had stopped on the sidewalk and seemed transfixed by something they saw down the street.

Stuart whistled. "I don't believe it," he said. "A vintage Citroën. Hydropneumatic suspension. Mint condition too."

I read the license plate. *Je me souviens*: I remember. The car was from Québec.

Brian nodded. "Early 1970s? Haven't seen one of those in years. I wonder who owns it."

As if on cue, the low, round sedan, dropped softly down to the ground as the suspension let out air. The driver's door opened. A tall man in a leather jacket emerged, as sophisticated as the car he drove and, in Gasper's Cove, just as exotic. One hand lifted to smooth curly brown hair, the other to straighten the perfect lapels of the jacket.

Our visitor strolled toward us, confident and easy. As he got closer, I noticed that his hair was expensively cut, longer than local men wore it, so it curled at the temples and grazed his collar. A few steps away, he reached up and removed his aviator sunglasses. I was startled to see how blue his eyes were, faceted like cracked glass. "Handsome like a movie star," my mother would have said, and she would have been right. I was sorry that Darlene, still trapped in investigative detainment, was not here to see this.

I caught my breath. Stuart noticed.

"Quite the car you've got there," Stuart said. "What is it? An SM?"

"DS, actually," the stranger replied. "The same model the police used in France. Not quite as famous as the

Traction Avant, but the best a nostalgic old cop from Québec could find."

A cop? But not old, I thought, not at all. My age, at least.

"Police?" Brian was alert. "What brings you here?"

"Excuse me," the man from Québec put out his hand. "Gilles DeWolf, senior media relations officer, Royal Canadian Mounted Police. Here in this beautiful place, half on business, half *en vacances*. I had a good excuse for a road trip." He paused and looked directly at me. "And *Madame*, who am I to resist?"

That was it. Where was Darlene when I needed her? Not only did this one look like a movie star; he sounded like one too. I heard Stuart clear his throat as he reached out to shake the man's hand.

"Stuart Campbell. Local engineer and campaign manager for this character"—he nodded toward Brian—"who is running for mayor. You'll see the signs around town. Brian Nickerson," he added, as if to elevate Brian's significance, and maybe his own.

And my signs, I thought, you'll see beside dead bodies. I didn't say that out loud. Instead, I introduced myself.

"I'm Valerie Rankin. That's our family store down the street. I manage it, and the campaign for our next mayor, Darlene Mowat." I wanted to jab Stuart in the side, but this comment was the best I could do.

"Ah, competitors," DeWolf said, the skin around those staggering eyes crinkling with amusement. "I will have to be careful not to get into the middle of this."

Stuart grunted. I ignored him.

"DeWolf? Any relation to the DeWolfs on Isle Madame?" I asked, referring to a small but spectacular island on the lower eastern coast of Cape Breton.

Gilles drew back his head and laughed. "Yes, my grandfather was from Isle Madame," he said. "He left to go to Québec to work in the mills. When my business here is wrapped up, I am going to take a drive down there and look around."

Brian stepped forward. "Media relations? National? Sounds interesting." He studied the newcomer carefully. "What is your business here, exactly?"

Gilles smiled slightly and looked through the window into the Agapi. "Right now, my business is lunch. It was a pleasure to meet you," he said, nodding to me, ignoring the men. "I will look forward to seeing you again."

Stuart stepped in front of me.

"A car like that," he said. "It must be hard to find parts."

"No, not at all," Gilles said with a shrug. "It is always possible to find anything. You just need to know where to look."

CHAPTER EIGHT

After our meeting with the movie star, I left the two old college roommates on the sidewalk. I then headed down the street to the store and the sanity of my sewing classroom.

The truth was, seeing Stuart and Brian together bothered me. I had no right to feel this way. Stuart was his own person, and I was mine. Still, I had started to feel that we were like two small boats, sailing in parallel, hulls briefly touching, but somehow headed to the same port. This stupid division between us for politics, something I didn't even believe in, felt like a betrayal. On an irrational level, his rejection of Darlene's candidacy felt like a rejection of me. It reminded me of the differences between us, the professional engineer and the small-town sewing teacher. It was as if he were saying, "Don't forget, I come from better, and I can do better. And I have the ring to prove it."

It hurt, but when I walked through the old doors of Rankin's General, I put it behind me. On the other side of this threshold, there were no politics, no rivalries, no conflicts, and no unsolved murders. Here, the world was steady. Here, I could walk on the same worn boards my ancestors had walked on, through two world wars, the Great Depression, the last of the sailing ships, and the decline of the fisheries. Within these walls, they had survived. Often, I knew, their worst days had been followed by their best ones. Whenever life got hard, I would always think, *Get me back to the store. I will be fine there. I am a Rankin.*

And now, the store was mine to run.

It had been nearly a year since Rollie left. At first, I had worked around his old edges, leaving the manager's office in chaos and the aisles illogical, tools interrupted by homewares, gardening supplies down a dead end past plumbing. Over time, I had eased in and returned the store to its roots. If it was a quality product and useful, we carried it. If it wasn't, we marked it down and moved it out. "As Seen on TV" had been replaced by "Buy Local." I had also expanded the sewing classroom and begun to offer workshops for our summer residents. Duck Macdonald, our handyman, converted the closet to a changing room. He also put a couch and coffee urn outside the classroom door for break times and chats. I had big plans.

I knew that Rankin's General needed to change to survive. As manager, I had looked at the books. Many months, the business upstairs in the Co-op brought in more than the hardware downstairs. It was clear that creativity was our best product. Once they'd been to Gasper's Cove, many of the tourists came back. Some came to stay and retire, some to build, and some to buy summer homes. These new residents had money, they liked crafts, and they wanted to learn how to do things themselves. We were our own resource. Why not populate the island with creative people? Why not run classes, schools, and retreats?

Brian Nickerson and Elliot Carter might have their plans for Gasper's Cove, I thought as I walked down the aisles. *I had mine.*

My scheming was interrupted by a wobbling bucket of mops. This wasn't usual for mops. I looked closer. Behind them, I saw a small man crouched low in the corner.

I recognized him at once.

"Harry Sutherland? What are you doing back there?" Harry was a familiar figure in the town. At one time, he had been a town councillor, until a gambling habit got in the way. Now, he ran the Zamboni ice resurfacer at the rink in the winter and managed a small garden center and the yacht club in the summer.

Harry pulled apart the strings of the mopheads and looked carefully out. "Is he gone?" he asked. "The commodore, is he gone?"

I looked around. All I could see was the scrawny back end of Elliot Carter exiting the store. "I don't know who you're talking about," I said. "No one else here. Mr. Carter just left."

Harry stepped into the aisle, relief on his face. "That was a close one," he said. "Nice mops."

"Don't change the subject, Harry," I ordered. "Who's the commodore?"

"Carter. Don't you know the story?" he asked.

I shook my head.

Harry continued. "When he first moved here, Carter applied to be the president of the yacht club. He had a nice boat, so we said, why not?" The Gasper's Cove yacht club was not exactly as advertised. Mostly, it was a collection of retired lobster boats recommissioned for recreational use and small cabin sailboats of 30 feet and under. The club president, as far as I knew, was responsible for not much more than buying the occasional round of drinks.

"How's that a problem?" I asked. "And why were you hiding?"

"You don't understand," Harry looked nervous again. "As soon as he was elected, Carter went nuts. He insisted we call him 'commodore,' not 'association president.' Then, he wanted a reserved parking space, with a sign. But the worst was when he wanted me to paint his position on the mooring buoy for his boat." Harry stopped and looked at me. "There are nine letters in *commodore*. You try painting that on a two-foot plastic bubble, without using hyphens. It's no joke."

I could see his point. "That's why you were avoiding him? He's too much work?"

"A pain more like it," Harry said, leaning closer. "You know why we got stuck with him here, don't you? I have a buddy with a good job in the government down in Halifax, and he told me something. My buddy works in motor vehicles, at the license renewal counter. In a position like that, you hear a lot."

I could only imagine. "Like what?"

Harry looked around for eavesdroppers. "He said Carter had applied to be a department head across the civil service for years. He was stuck at Public Works. But whenever he applied anywhere else, he got passed over. It got to be a joke. They said he didn't care what the job was, he just wanted to be the head of something. The word is he moved here because we were the only place dumb enough to offer him a title." Harry snickered. "Here, he's finally a director and a commodore. Now with this election thing, he's trying to be a 'Your Worship.'" Harry shook his head. "You know what they say?"

I didn't, at least not in Harry's world.

"The only man who needs a title that bad is one who doesn't have friends." Harry paused to hitch up his pants. "That's why I never chase fancy positions myself. I've got dozens of friends, maybe hundreds, probably close to a thousand. Status is not something I need." He winked. "If a fellow like Carter doesn't have something important to call himself, he's got nothing."

Harry reached over and picked up a mop. "I bet my mom would like one of these," he said, then checked the price tag. "Give me a discount? As a friend?"

CHAPTER NINE

I took Harry to the front cash and explained to Colleen that we were giving him the mop at 10 percent off. Colleen was Darlene's mother. Like her daughter, she had opinions of her own. Colleen sighed dramatically at me but rang him up.

"You'll never make any money doing that," she said after Harry left. "People take advantage of you. Look what that Carter fellow tried on me just now. Claimed he forgot his wallet, to put it on his tab. I told him to go home and get his money. We'd still be here."

"I didn't even know that he had a tab," I said. Where was that written down?

"Yes, it was something Rollie set up. He called it a 'gentleman's agreement.' Well, no gentlemen here now, are there? Except Duck, and he's one of us," she said, counting the bills in the cash register. "The Elliots of the world better get used to it."

Colleen stopped talking. She stared past my shoulder to look out the front window, her mouth open. I turned around.

An RCMP cruiser was in front of the store. Wade Corkum was behind the wheel, and right next to him, in the passenger's seat, was Darlene.

"What in the world ...," Colleen said. "There's my girl!"

Together, we ran through the doors and onto the sidewalk. By the time I got there, Darlene was already out of the car. She took off her sunglasses and hugged us.

"I've been sprung," she said. "We're back in business."

"You have? What happened?" Colleen hugged Darlene. She was ecstatic. Some of her other children, the boys, had been arrested, but this time was the first that one had been returned, delivered door to door.

The driver's door slammed. Wade walked over.

"No reason to hold her," he said to Colleen, studying the sidewalk. "Results came in from the lab in Drummond. They verified that the hair wasn't Darlene's."

"I told you so," my cousin said. "Tell her, Wade, tell her whose red hair it was."

Wade picked up a speck of something from the ground and studied it. "It was confirmed as canine. They said they knew right away. Dog hair is thicker, the color pattern is not the same, very different than human hair," Wade mumbled. "They figure it was from a golden retriever."

"Do you believe it?" Darlene asked her mother. "I spent all this time with the RCMP because there were dog hairs, Toby's hairs, on a sign made at Valerie's house. You know, the house covered from one end to the other in dog hair?"

That was not true—not from one end to the other. I kept the door to the spare room closed. Wade didn't say anything. He was busy studying the concrete joints in the curb.

"An honest mistake," I said to him out of pity. Darlene laughed. "What happens now?"

"I'm going home," Darlene answered. "I've got to have a hot bath, talk to my cats, and get back to running for mayor. This town needs someone who knows what they're doing," she added, giving Wade a sideways look. "I got dropped off here to see Mom. My car's out back."

"Wait 'til I tell the crafters," I said. I was vacuuming tonight, that was for sure. No one was coming back into my house until I did.

Darlene detached herself from her mother's arms. Still giggling, Darlene and Colleen headed to the parking lot behind the store. I turned to follow them. Wade put out a hand.

"Valerie, I would like a word with you, in private, if you have the time," he said. "Why don't we go for a little drive?"

I was wary. Wade and I hadn't had a personal conversation since high school. I couldn't imagine why he wanted to talk to me now, but I was curious. So, when Wade opened the passenger door of the cruiser, I slid into the seat Darlene had just left. We headed out of town.

$\sim$

As soon as we left Gasper's Cove behind, I realized that Wade was taking me to the look-off on Shore Road. This conversation was going to be serious. The local look-off was the standby venue for important private conversations, such as confessions, marriage proposals, and breakups. In our case, I suspected that we were going there to discuss a murder. Wade drove carefully, sweeping his eyes left and right as we headed out of town, as if afraid we would be seen.

After he swung into the parking lot, with its spectacular view of the ocean, Wade pulled over as far away as he could from the other cars. I waited for him to start.

"This is between us," he said. He opened a package of Juicy Fruit gum and offered me a stick. I shook my head. "It goes no further. It's about all these things going on." He looked at the horizon. "It's a lot."

I'd seen that face before. In algebra class. A tall skinny boy with chalk in his hand and no idea what the equation on the blackboard meant.

"I can imagine," I said. "A dead former mayor. A current candidate in detention over dog hair. You've got a full plate."

"Val, don't make fun of me. You know the local stuff. That's just half of it. It gets worse." Wade took off his hat. I could see the sweat on his bald head. "I've got my hands full here, and now I have that stupid report to deal with. Why did that crazy professor write that paper? I can't fail."

"It's just a theory. No one's going to take him seriously," I said. "I mean, really? Productive gossip?"

"Oh, he's serious all right." The sweat was running down the sides of Wade's head in meandering streams. He pulled out a handkerchief from under his padded vest. "He says the clan system brought it over from Scotland. He says that it's why we can't let anything go. Why we solve crimes."

"Is that a problem?" I asked him. "Aren't you getting an award? Doesn't this make you look good?"

"Maybe too good," Wade said. "The expectations are high. I haven't been under pressure like this since the AAA provincials in hockey, and I thought that was as tough as it got." He lowered his window for air. "Have you met the PR guy the brass sent down?"

How could I forget?

"I might have," I said.

"He's here to get ready for some presentation thing, bring in the media, commend me for my great detective work." Wade's voice was a croak.

"Congratulations," I said, "but again, what's wrong with that?"

"Lots," Wade squirmed in his seat. "Right now, with Mike, we have an unsolved murder. I'm supposed to show everyone how I handle it. Truth is, I am not sure how I did it before. Maybe the professor is right. The community sort of helped. Look, when I try to do this on my own, I end up covered in dog hair."

Wade stirred uncomfortably in the seat next to me. I stayed quiet, not sure whether I was ready to hear where this conversation was going.

"Why am I here?" I asked.

Wade pulled his eyes away from the view through his windshield and looked at me.

"I have a request to make, in confidence, to you as a member of the public," he said. "Someone who gets in the middle of everything."

I sat up. In the past, any official interaction I had with Wade had resulted in his telling me to stop being a nuisance. Was that about to change? Was he asking for my assistance? My day got brighter.

Wade seemed to read my mind.

"Don't get too excited, Valerie. I wouldn't be here if I didn't have this DeWolf guy looking over my shoulder. I have sent Officer Nolan off to handle our other calls so I can concentrate on this case. I am trying to figure out what to do next." He hesitated, then spoke quickly, as if to get the words out before he could take them back. "If you run across anything that seems unusual, could you tell me? I'll decide if it is worth following up. Make sense?"

Yes, it made sense. I traveled in a lot of circles Wade didn't, and everyone in my circles was a talker. There wasn't much that went on in Gasper's Cove, or even in Drummond, that I didn't hear about. I felt deputized.

"Does this mean I am sort of an undercover agent for the RCMP?" I asked, hearing the thrill in my voice.

Wade put his sweaty head down on the steering wheel and took a few deep breaths, as if to calm himself. "No, it does not, and if you tell anyone about this ... "

I knew what he was trying to say. "My lips are sealed, and my eyes are open, Officer Corkum. I'll report directly to you."

Wade lifted his head, put the car in gear, and backed out onto the road to town. "Don't make me regret this conversation," he said. "Just, don't."

CHAPTER TEN

When Wade dropped me off at the store, I was surprised to see that Darlene's car was still in the back lot. What about her bath? Why wasn't she at home with her cats?

As soon as I walked through the doors, I had my answer. School was done for the day, and teen Polly, our unofficial volunteer strategist, was at the front counter. Her laptop was open beside the cash register. Darlene and Colleen were next to her, peering at the screen.

"While you were in detention, I put all the action items from that women candidates pamphlet on a spreadsheet," Polly explained to Darlene. "I also looked at the other campaigns, as benchmarks."

"Is that fair to us?" I asked her. "They have budgets, and we don't."

Darlene held up a palm. "Wait. Don't panic. Polly has it all worked out."

I walked behind the counter to look at the document on the laptop. Darlene was right—there it was. Everything we needed to do, including how we were going to do it:

1. Phone bank. (Charlie: a rotary phone at home. Brian: paid service. Elliot: municipal employee "volunteers"). Us: Seaview Manor Senior Ladies Bridge Club. Point person: Grandma Brown.

2. Campaign literature distribution. (Charlie: doesn't believe in paper signs and recycles brochures. Brian and Elliot: postage paid and sent out by Canada Post). Us: Local dog walkers. Small breeds, flat streets; large breeds, hilly streets. Point person: Toby and Valerie Rankin.

3. Campaign vehicle. (Charlie: his bike, new tires. Brian: Van, custom painted in Halifax. Elliot: His truck with magnetic signs.) Us: Appliqué flags for Valerie's and Darlene's cars. Made by the quilter's guild, materials donated by Annette.

4. Fundraising. (Charlie: fiddle-case donations when he plays at the market on Saturdays. Elliot: $50-a-plate dinner at Gasper's Cove Yacht Club, speaker Elliot Carter. Brian: $200-a-plate dinner at Chisholm House, Drummond. Speakers: The Honorable Len Clayton, Member of the Nova Scotia House of Assembly; the Honorable Vincent Dunbrack, Member of the Parliament of Canada; and Senator the Honorable Scott Lindsay.) Us: Bake sale table, Rankin's General Store, Gasper's Cove.

5. Media relations. (Charlie: boycotting all mass media. Elliot: Slipstream Communications, Halifax. Brian: McKenna, McKenna, and McKenna Media Relations London, New York, and Toronto). Us: Sarah Chisholm, prosthetic technician, Drummond Consolidated Hospital; Polly Brown, final-year student, Gasper's Cove Junior High School.

I was impressed. Ours would be the real campaign—the voters of Gasper's Cove would see that. Polly and I bumped fists. Our junior executive had come through again.

"Just let them try to stop us now," Colleen said. "We're ready for whatever they throw at us."

She was wrong.

⌒ᴏ⌒

As I stood at the counter with my best friend and employees, old and young, I felt a rush of air as the door to the store opened. Noah walked in. He wore jeans, not washed this month, work boots, a T-shirt, a plaid jacket, and a backpack. If it weren't for the recorder in his hands, he could be mistaken for any other surfer or student. But Noah was here on business.

"Hey, Valerie. Thought I would find you here," he nodded to my cousin. "And Darlene. A bonus. Time for a quick statement? On the record?" Noah's thumb was already on a button of the recorder.

"Sure," Darlene said, smiling a little too brightly. "As a responsible citizen, I have just returned from a consultation with the RCMP. All part of my commitment to finding Mike's killer. Unfortunately, I wasn't able to help the Mounties as much as I wanted."

I looked at my cousin. Who knew that the provincial updo champion was also such a great spin doctor? Darlene was catching on.

So was Noah.

"Excellent, but that's not what I want to talk to you about," he said.

"It isn't?" I asked, walking out from behind the counter. My campaign manager's spidey senses were tingling. Something was up.

Noah reached into his backpack and pulled out a sheet of paper. He handed it to me. It was a press release. Darlene and Colleen leaned over to read it with us.

The logo at the top said that it was from the Brian Nickerson for Mayor Campaign. Briefly, I wondered whether Stuart had written it.

DRUMMOND, Nova Scotia—Well-known lawyer and candidate for mayor Brian Nickerson has called for a public debate on policy issues with his chief competitor in the race, former deputy mayor Elliot Carter. Recent polls show Nickerson and Carter with 36% and 33% support, respectively, among decided voters. Gasper's Cove hair stylist Darlene Mowat trails with 17% support, and frequent candidate Charlie Landry with 1%. Thirteen percent of eligible voters remain undecided.

"It's clear that this is a two-person race," says Nickerson. "The people of our community have a right to know where we each stand on the issues: local, provincial, and national. I can think of no better way to do that than at a public meeting. Accountability matters."

The Carter campaign has accepted Nickerson's invitation to the debate, which will be held at 8:00 pm this Saturday at the Drummond Civic Center. All are invited to attend.

It took me a minute to absorb the meaning of the release. When I did, I was furious.

"They're having a debate, and we're not invited?" Darlene asked Noah. "The arrogant jerks."

I glared at Noah. "Turn that thing off," I ordered in my best mother's voice, looking at the recorder. "Give us a minute to think of a response. What are the other candidates saying?"

Noah pulled a well-worn notebook out of his backpack. It was probably the same one he had used in high school. I resisted the impulse to ask him whether he wanted me to sign his homework.

"Let's see here," he said. "Landry is going to protest. He's down at the Civic Center setting up. Something about a hunger strike."

"And Elliot?" Darlene asked. "He's in on it too. What did he say about us being shut out like this?"

Noah studied a page, avoiding our eyes.

"He had nice things to say about you, Darlene, and your group," he stammered. "He commended you for your enthusiasm."

"That's not all, is it?" I asked. "Come on, Noah, spit it out."

"He pointed out how well-qualified he is, and that government is no place for amateurs." Noah looked over to Polly, as the next youngest person in the vicinity, for support. She crossed her arms and glared at him.

Beside me, I could feel the heat begin to radiate off Darlene's body. Never call a redhead an amateur. I put my hand on Darlene's arm. If she was going to explode, it shouldn't be in front of a reporter.

"Continue," I said. There was more. If there is one thing I know, it's when a kid isn't telling me everything.

"You sure?" Noah asked, unexpectedly nervous. "He said he appreciated your interest, but that ... "—he read carefully—"in his words, 'Maybe the ladies from that craft co-op should stick to their knitting.'" The young reporter swallowed. "Any comment?"

I tightened my grip on Darlene's arm. She pushed my hand away.

"No comment," she said. "We'll make our own news. Watch for it."

CHAPTER ELEVEN

The Drummond Civic Center was also the local hockey arena, converted for events like the debate with insulated plywood laid over the ice. Tonight, the glass walls used to protect spectators from flying pucks were down. Rough players had been replaced by campaign literature in the penalty box.

From our chilly seats in front of the stage, Darlene, the crafters, and I had the best view. Sylvie was a genius.

At the meeting at my house two nights before, she had come up with a plan. The debate was open to the public and that, she reasoned, included us. Tilly Ferguson and her friends arranged our first-row seats, right where Elliot and Brian couldn't avoid our faces. Many of the ushers were crafters' grandchildren. Tonight, we had been led into the arena like royalty.

Our seats were right next to the media table, the riser for cameras, and the standing microphone set up for questions from the audience. I was surprised to see so many reporters. I wondered what strings Brian had pulled to get them here.

A gaggle of camera operators had even been outside the front doors when we arrived. They had filmed Charlie at his post, six hours into his hunger strike and already looking weak. Now, they, like us, waited for the event to begin.

Part of the delay was caused by the arrival of the larger-than-expected Nickerson entourage—Brian's father, the senator; two MPs from Ottawa; a member of the provincial House of Assembly; Stuart; and right behind him, two men, better dressed than the rest and less talkative.

"Who are those guys?" I asked Darlene, pointing behind my hand to the quiet pair.

Darlene peered over. "Oh, them," she said dismissively. "Party bagmen. Developers from Ontario."

Unlike the two businessmen, the politicians took their time marching down the center aisle, waving and shaking hands, only to arrive at the front and see the seats that they had assumed were for them were taken. The group covered their surprise with good-natured bluster and jostled into the row behind us, but not before exchanging shrewd looks. These men were pros. They knew that something was up, and they didn't like it.

We let them wonder, biding our time.

Brian spoke first.

Predictably, he talked about progress and prosperity as if they were the same thing. He also spoke of how amalgamation was a model for the whole country, which made no sense at all. Finally, he asked for a moment of silence for the late, great, Mighty Mike Murphy, who, Brian was sure, was proud of us now. When he was done, the row behind us clapped. A few reached over to pat Brian's father on the back.

Elliot Carter was next.

Elliot stood up, walked to the microphone, and swabbed it with an antibacterial wipe. He cleared his throat and opened his mouth to speak.

This was our moment.

In one motion, with discipline and coordination that made me proud, the crafters, Darlene, and I reached under our seats and pulled out our knitting. Then, holding our turquoise scarves, socks, and mittens up high for the cameras, we started to knit. The people in the seats near us giggled. A few in the rows behind us laughed. Men at the back whistled. The women next to them clapped. I heard the click of the cameras as they were taken off the tripods and carried closer for a better shot. Up on the stage, Brian Nickerson smirked. Behind me, Stuart whispered, "Good one."

Elliot Carter glared down at us, his pale face even more translucent than normal. Trembling with anger, he reached into his pocket, pulled out a paper, and tightened his grip on the mic.

"Nice stunt, *ladies*," he said, making things worse. "But unfortunately, you need more than theatrics to run a municipality. You need fiscal responsibility. Shall we talk about that?"

"Bring it on," Sylvie hooted. She hadn't had this much fun since she'd learned to batik dye.

"Happy to," Elliot said, pulling a pair of wireless glasses out of his pocket and sliding them onto his featureless face. "Let's look at Darlene Mowat's discretionary spending from her time as a councillor in Gasper's Cove. I have the numbers right here." Elliot waved the papers in his hand at the audience, as if they could read his evidence. He peered over the top of his glasses and held up a finger.

"One: handrail for the ramp at the playground?" Elliot turned his finger down to point directly at Darlene. "These are children. What was that for?"

Tilly was on her feet. "The seniors," she said loudly. "Some of the ladies like to go down and watch the children play on a sunny day. We don't want any falls," she added as she sat down. There was a murmur of approval from around the arena.

"Right," Elliot said. We'd caught him off guard, but he was quick to regroup. "Valentine's Day dinner? $2,000? How is that a civic responsibility? Misuse of public funds." Elliot took off his glasses, stared at Darlene, and walked closer to the cameras.

A big man, one of the local fishermen, stepped up to the public microphone.

"The widows," he called out.

"Excuse me?" Elliot said. "I fail to see what they have to do with Valentine's Day."

"Everything," an older woman said, making her way over to stand beside the fisherman. "It was Darlene's idea. Something special for all of us ladies who've lost our husbands. She's organized handsome men like this fellow here"—she nudged the fisherman with her cane—"to come to our doors, in suits, with corsages of real flowers. Drive us down to the hall for a special Valentine's Day dinner." She turned to beam at Darlene. "What's wrong with that?"

Elliot stood stiffly in front of the audience, silenced by embarrassment and rage. Brian, catching a nod from his father, walked over and wrestled the microphone from Elliot's tight fist.

"Nothing wrong with that at all," Brian said, stepping in front of his competitor. "This is a program my administration will support and," he paused dramatically, "expand. Another reflection of the spirit of caring central to my vision for this great nation of ours."

"Great nation?" Sylvie whispered to me. "What is he talking about? It's a dinner for old ladies in a church hall."

I heard her and nodded but didn't respond. Instead, I studied the stage. I tried to see the scene in front of me like Wade would, with his policeman's eyes, with a murder to solve. What would he see? Two men running in an election that had five contenders a week ago. In addition to those on the stage, one was now dead, one was knitting, and one was hungry on the sidewalk outside.

Two men.

I didn't really know either of them. My intelligence on Elliot the wanna-be commodore came from behind a mop. I knew more about Brian's ring than I did about him. The suits behind me stirred. Folding chairs creaked under well-nourished weight. Charlie had fled a prosperous family in Boston to avoid becoming a man like they were. He had found his place here. Darlene was trying to save it. Those were motivations I could understand. But what about the candidates on stage?

Then, I remembered. Charlie at the Agapi, his big hand holding a tiny cup. What had he told me about politics?

Ego and ambition.

Well, there they were, in person, right in front of me on the debate stage.

One of each.
Ego and ambition.
But which was the more dangerous?

CHAPTER TWELVE

Crafty Candidate Crashes and Crushes Competition

The photo underneath the caption in the next morning's *Lighthouse Online* said it all. There we were, a row of bratty knitters. Behind us, in the background, were the blurred faces of Brian and Elliot. We had made our point. It was unlikely that Darlene would be shut out of any other public events.

There was a lesson here. Sticking to our knitting was exactly what we should do. The pressure of public life, if you counted rural politics as public life, could make a person start acting the way other people expected. But the real power lay in remaining who you were.

Crafting and sewing had taught me this lesson. Who had decided that working with your hands was less significant than working with your head? Maybe one day, a professor would write a paper about that topic.

My best ideas came when I was sewing. The predictable regularity of stitches marching out from under a presser foot steadied my nerves. The act of taking nothing but a paper pattern, flat fabric, and a spool of thread and making something of it built hope into my life. How did people who didn't make things manage without this gift? How many times had I stood in the Co-op, as I was today, and had visitors ask me, "How do you find the time?" How could I ever explain that for a person like me, there was no choice?

Gilles DeWolf understood.

He'd come into the Co-op early and been there for more than an hour, his phone out, taking pictures of everything we sold, asking questions, and handing me what he wanted to buy.

I was curious.

"You've got quite a selection here. Gifts? Family?" *Maybe a wife at home,* I wanted to ask.

Gilles smiled and added a cross-stitched apron to the pile. I hadn't fooled him. "Aunts, nieces, a colleague or two. I'm no longer married. The job."

He'd told me no more than he had to, but it was what I wanted to know.

I changed the subject. "Do you make things?" I asked. "You have an eye for detail."

Gilles shrugged. "No, not me, but I admire those who can. There's some excellent work here." He held up his phone. "That's why I am taking pictures. Who knows, some of you might be famous one day. I can say I discovered you."

I suddenly felt like I needed to open the window. It was warm up here on the second floor. An old building, poor ventilation, sometimes that happened.

I took Gilles's credit card, and our hands briefly touched. I heard voices at the bottom of the stairs on the main floor. I moved my hand away.

"One more thing," Gilles said. "For my job." He leaned over the counter. Up close, I could see how perfect his teeth were. "I need some background for the preparations to recognize an outstanding officer. I would like to know more about the community. Can you help me?"

I was flattered. When was the last time anyone wanted my opinion? "Whatever you need to know," I said.

"Excellent," Gilles paused. "I have an idea. How about dinner?"

Really? I wasn't expecting this.

"That would be nice," I said. "There is the Agapi here in Gasper's, and the Peking Palace over in Drummond ... "

"Actually, I was thinking of cooking for you," Gilles said. "If you'd allow me. What do you think?"

I panicked.

In my house? In my dog hair–covered, tiny bungalow with its un-renovated kitchen with the avocado-green stove? In my house, with Aunt Dot's sculpted carpet in the living room and fluffy pink toilet seat cover in the bathroom?

I would need a new filter for the vacuum. I would have to wash the baseboards, clean the oven, iron a tablecloth, and scrub out the fridge.

"Sounds great," I said using my relaxed yoga-like voice. I should start yoga. "When were you thinking?" I asked, hoping to buy time. "What will you need?"

"Friday?" Gilles asked. "Don't worry. I'll bring everything. All you have to do is relax, let me cook, and talk to me. Say, six o'clock?"

Candles. I could get some at the Foodmart. I'd bathe Toby. What would I wear?

"I think I'm free Friday night," I said. *Like every Friday night*, I could have added, but didn't. "That sounds nice. Let me give you the address."

Gilles smiled. "No need. I know where you are." He picked up his bag from the counter. "See you Friday."

"Looking forward to it," I said. I was.

As Gilles went down the stairs, he passed our next customer on the way up. It was Stuart.

"What's that guy doing here?" he asked.

"Shopping, what else?" I answered. Stuart had broken the mood. I was vaguely annoyed. "How about you? Looking for some embroidered tea towels? Driftwood bookends?"

"Neither," he said, handing me a small poster. "Erin asked me to drop this off and see whether you would put it up in the store. Also, she'd like you to come."

I smiled. Stuart's daughter, Erin, was one of my favorite people. She reminded me of myself at that age, flustered, artistic, and compelled to create. She and Polly made friendship bracelets and earrings we sold in the Co-op.

I picked up the paper and read it. It was for the Gasper's Cove Junior High Young Entrepreneurs Fair. Erin and Polly had a table. Doors would open to the public at two o'clock Monday afternoon.

This event was about kids—it mattered. "Tell her I will be there. And I'll put up her poster in the window. I'm proud of them."

"Thanks, appreciate it," Stuart said. I thought that he was going to leave, but he stayed in front of the counter. He looked at the pressed-metal ceiling above us as though he had never seen it before.

"There's one other thing," he said. "A message from Brian."

I could feel my earlier annoyance return.

"If Brian has something to say, why doesn't he say it himself?" I asked.

"To be honest, he thought you might be more receptive to this coming from me," Stuart said.

"He did, did he? What is this thing he's afraid to tell me?"

Stuart stopped looking at the ceiling and moved over to the big semicircular window to stare out at the water. He had seen the water before.

"You did well with the crowd last night, Val. That was a pretty slick move," Stuart said. "It got noticed."

Meaning that Brian's dear old dad and his friends took notice, I thought. I wondered where this was going.

Stuart turned to face me.

"Brian wonders if Darlene would be interested in becoming his deputy mayor when he's elected," he said. "She'd have all the power she needs to do what she wants without any of the bruising that comes with an election."

I got it now. "Are you asking what I think you're asking?"

Stuart wouldn't look me in the eyes. "She'd have to withdraw from the race and endorse Brian," he said. "I mean, it's not like she's got a chance with this thing, so why not?"

"No," I said. "I don't even have to ask her. The answer is no. Brian found out last night that Darlene is popular. He wants some of that. Tough bananas, it's not his. Go back to your boss and tell him to forget it."

Stuart stepped closer. "I wish you'd reconsider," he said. "I'll be honest. I don't like you so invested in this. I don't want to see you disappointed."

This was the wrong thing to say to me. The absolute wrong thing. "I can take care of myself," I retorted. "So can Darlene."

Stuart wasn't giving up. "Look what happened to Mike. It would be foolish to say that it had nothing to do with politics. I nearly had a stroke when I heard that you had found his body. I don't like you close to something like that. What's wrong with doing what you were doing? Running the store, the Co-op, and teaching your classes?"

I looked at Stuart for so long that it made him uncomfortable. Who was he to want me to stay the same? Who was he to tell Darlene not to take a stand for what mattered to her?

Did Stuart forget who we were and where we came from? Our grandmother had gotten out of bed and gone downstairs to put in a last load of laundry on the morning she'd died. No one was going to tell her granddaughters what they couldn't do.

I put my hands flat on the counter and straightened my back before stepping away. "I can't say I appreciate your concern. I don't," I said. "This is our town, and we're going to take care of it. Back us up or get out of our way." I looked around the Co-op at all the careful, clever things the crafters had made.

"If there's anything here I can sell you, I'd be happy to help you out," I said. "Otherwise, I have things to do."

Stuart hesitated, then turned and left. There was nothing else for either of us to say.

CHAPTER THIRTEEN

The minute Stuart was gone, I called Darlene.

"That Gilles guy from *La Belle Province* was here," I said. "He's coming over to the house Friday to cook me dinner."

"No way!" Darlene responded. "I've seen him around. He's hot."

"Do you think?" I asked. "He only wants to talk. Some PR thing about the community. But listen—what am I going to wear?"

Darlene's answer was automatic. "Slides on your feet. Loose pants, tight top. Cleavage, messy bun. Little bit of sparkle in the jewelry."

"Sounds like you've done this a lot."

"I have."

"Makeup?"

"Keep the lips light, work on your eyes. Eyeliner. But don't make it look like you tried too hard."

"Perfume?"

"Where's he from again?"

"Montreal."

"Then, yes, definitely."

"Thanks, this helps," I said.

"Hang on," Darlene said. "Clean the house. Vacuum. The dog hair. He'll probably wear black."

"Got it." I'd move the dog bed out of the living room. "That's it?"

"If I think of anything else, I'll let you know," my cousin said. "We can talk when we canvass."

We didn't want to canvass. The idea of knocking on people's doors and asking for their vote seemed rude. But this game was the one we'd signed up for, so off we went.

Because we already knew everyone in Gasper's Cove, we decided to cross the causeway to Drummond to practice our canvassing in a new subdivision.

It didn't take long to realize that this territory was not friendly. The first street we visited, called Horseshoe Drive, for obvious reasons, was already plastered with signs for Brian and Elliot. Darlene was undeterred.

"Maybe they're just being polite," she said. "They could be relatives. The worst we can do today is have a chat."

The first door was opened by a man in his seventies.

He smiled at Darlene. Then, he saw the campaign button on her dress.

"Not interested," he said, pointing to Elliot's sign on his lawn. "I'm going with Mike's guy."

"Your wife in?" Darlene asked, before the door closed.

We worked our way down the street like that, leaving a few signs of our own, buying juice from two giggling girls for 25 cents, and helping retrieve an indoor cat that had escaped to hide under a bush.

We were at the end of the horseshoe, back where we had started, when I noticed a sign next to a small bungalow: "Syd's Repairs, Autobody, and Towing." There was a smaller handwritten sign below it: "Out back."

"Let's go around," I suggested. I needed a mechanic. My car wasn't getting better on its own. We made our way down the driveway to a three-door garage behind the house. A large middle-aged man, his paint- and grease-stained overalls straining over a wide belly, came out to meet us.

"Can I help you, ladies?" he asked, looking over our shoulders to see whether a man, or at least a vehicle, was behind us.

Darlene put on her best candidate smile and stuck out her hand. "I'm Darlene Mowat. I'm running for mayor."

The man shoved his own hands deep into his pockets. "Syd Johnson," he said curtly. "I don't vote."

"Why's that?" I asked. Fielding opposition was my job.

"Had enough of crooks working with Mighty Mike," he said. "I boxed for him in the old days."

"Is that a fact?" Darlene asked. "What was that like?"

Syd laughed, but not with his eyes. "I took the hits, he took the cut. I got away from that guy while I was still in one piece."

I'd never talked to a boxer before. I was out of conversational ideas. Instead, I looked into the open door of the garage. Amazingly, given the old beater of a man in front of us, his work area was pristine. I identified a baby blue Pontiac GTO on the hoist and beside it a gold Buick LeSabre with the hood up. Syd Johnson knew what he was doing. I'd have to keep looking for a mechanic I could afford.

"Nice cars," Darlene said. "Too bad my brothers aren't here."

Syd smiled for the first time, exposing a mouthful of even, bright white implants. "Tell them if they like vintage cars to look me up. But," he said, giving her a shrewd look, "that still doesn't mean I'll vote for you. Don't mean to be rude, but all politicians are just in it for themselves. No patience for it."

⌒〇⌒

As soon as we were back at our car, Darlene announced that we needed Chinese food. After the trauma of door-to-door politicking, she figured that we'd earned the Peking Palace's #4 lunch special. We were halfway into our sweet-and-sour chicken balls when I brought up Brian's offer.

"Deputy mayor? Is he joking?" Darlene asked, choking. Fried rice flew across the table all the way to her Pepsi. "I hope Stuart felt bad suggesting it."

Oh yes, I thought, he felt bad. I'd seen to that. "Don't worry, I turned them down," I said.

"I should hope so." Darlene picked up a paper napkin. "What does Nickerson think? That he can acquire me and I'll deliver the Gasper's Cove vote? In his dreams."

"Getting votes isn't easy," I said. "Look at that guy with the baby blue GTO. He wasn't interested. Mint condition. I mean the car, not the guy."

Darlene snorted. "Custom paint job. That was a '67. Wrong shade of blue."

"You're kidding." Darlene's head was a junk drawer of random facts. "How do you even know that?"

"How many brothers do I have?" she asked.

"Five?"

"There's your answer right there," Darlene said, signaling for the check. "Drop me off at home. Don't you have a junior high fair to go to?"

I did. So, we left.

◦◦◦

It had been a long time since I had been inside a school. Walking on the polished floors, I was reminded of the parent-teacher interviews of my past. Most of the time, they had gone well. My daughter was always the perfect student, no trouble at all. My middle son spent too much time making his friends laugh. My youngest son paid more attention to his sports than to his studies. Parent-teacher interviews had always made me feel as though who was really being assessed was me as a single mother.

Being back in the same auditorium made me feel nervous. It was a relief to see the art teacher, Trevor Ross. He walked me over to the girls' display. A crowd was around their table. When we arrived, Erin was deep into a demonstration of the floss-knotting process, and Polly was handing out catalogs. I stretched up to see over the junior high heads and gave my protégées a thumbs-up. They grinned back at me.

"This is exciting for them," I said to Trevor. "Was the fair your idea?"

"It was," Trevor answered, pushing his slippery red glasses back up his nose. "You'd understand. I want the kids, and their parents, to see creative people can make a living."

"Preaching to the converted," I said. The whole area was packed with the activity of young bakers, plant growers, painters, and craftspeople. "This is so positive. People who make things undervalue themselves." I thought of the crafters at the debate, and then of Sylvie's sweater. "Look at Maud Lewis, our most famous folk artist. She sold *Three Black Cats* for a cheese sandwich."

Trevor looked away from me. He seemed uncomfortable. Had I offended him?

"You teach art, don't you?" I asked. "That must keep you busy."

"Yes, I do. But I also paint. Mainly for myself," he said, looking around. "Look, I should go," he said moving away from me. "I have students to see."

As I watched the art teacher scramble away, I felt a bony tap on my shoulder. I turned around and then wished I hadn't.

Elliot Carter was behind me. He pushed his phone close to my face.

"See this?" he asked. "You thought you were pretty clever last night, didn't you? Knitting away for a laugh. But numbers don't lie. No, sir. They never do."

I pushed Elliot's phone back so I could read it.

Catty Candidate's Cash Chaos

I thought the smirk on Elliot's face was as bad as the headline.

And then I read the article.

It was worse.

CHAPTER FOURTEEN

The byline in the *Lighthouse* said "Our staff."
They'd done their homework.

Information forwarded to this news outlet reveals
difficulties in candidate Darlene Mowat's financial past.
She has carried two second-mortgages on her home
and twice had her car in danger of repossession.

When asked to comment on Mowat's history,
Elliot Carter, campaigning for mayor on a platform
of fiscal responsibility, had this to say.

"I know Darlene's personal life has been complicated. There
were, what, three marriages?" he asked. "But that is irrelevant.
I wish Miss Mowat well. Being a hair stylist might not give a
person the training they need to handle municipal budgets."

When asked whether Mowat should withdraw from the
race, Carter said that it was not up to him to decide. "I
know people say she's in over her head, but I'm not one

of them," he said. "I admire the nerve it took for her
to run. I wish her well in her future endeavors."

Mowat's bank has declined to comment on her credit
history. Sources note, however, that Mowat obtained a new
car while dating Brett Cameron of Cameron Motors.

Mowat's campaign is being run by Valerie Rankin, manager
of Rankin's General Store. Rankin's own name has
been in the news. Readers might recall her ex-husband's
involvement in an embezzlement and harassment
scandal at his Halifax workplace 20 years ago.

I pushed the phone away.

"Oh, come on," Elliot said, his face as sympathetic as an
undertaker's. "I came to Darlene's defense. Not everyone has
my management record. I have an obligation to run. That's
why this one's for Mike."

"Yeah, right," I said. I looked around the auditorium. A
boy stood in front of a table of rainbow cupcakes. Did I have
enough money in my purse to buy them all and grind icing
into Elliot's face? He certainly could use the color.

I only had money for two. Ignoring Elliot, I handed the
student a dollar. I picked up a yellow and a pink cupcake
and left the auditorium. I'd sit in my car and eat them both.
Then, I would go home and see my dog. I needed to lean on
someone with integrity.

Behind the wheel of the car, and halfway through my
second cupcake, I had an idea. I dialed Noah's number.

Before I could even say hello, he apologized.

"I'm sorry. It wasn't my shift. I had no idea."

"Hope not," I countered. "Make it up to me. Tell me who wrote this garbage. I want to talk to them."

There was a pause. "You know I can't do that," he said. "Even if I knew. But you can leave a message. Just push '3' for the assignment editor. That will work."

"Thanks for your help," I said. I almost meant it.

I hung up and called the *Lighthouse Online*. I was led through several levels of recorded obstruction, during which I was repeatedly told that my call mattered. Eventually, I was invited to press 3.

I did.

I began by saying that I wanted to complain. I had no idea what that would mean, but it set the tone. I told the faceless assignment editor that the article about Darlene and me was unfair. I pointed out that these personal details were nobody's business. I asked why our campaign was the only one targeted.

I was cut off by a beep.

I called back. I wanted to use my last, best, most dramatic line.

"Everyone has secrets, everyone has a past," I told the listener at number 3. "I suggest that your staff look at the other candidates the way they looked at us. For sure, you'll find some stories there." I felt satisfied. This is how a real campaign manager would talk. I was sure of it. I tried to call back again to say that we had no further comment, but the mailbox was full.

I felt calmer. I had two cupcakes and the same number of angry phone messages under my belt. I headed home. I needed quiet. I needed peace. I needed to recover.

That wasn't going to happen.

The minute I pulled into my driveway, I could see my neighbor from across the street on the way over. Mrs. Smith took her assignment as Clark Drive's 24/7 one-person neighborhood watch very seriously.

She was in such a hurry that she crossed the street in her slippers.

"Valerie!" Mrs. Smith called as soon as she stepped off the curb. "There was a person!"

"There are people everywhere," I said. "Anyone in particular?"

"Someone had a clipboard and went around the side of your house like they were going to read the meter. That's when I started to wonder." Mrs. Smith could see that I was missing the point. "They checked your meter last week. First Tuesday of the month. Like usual."

I did not know that. Learn something new about your own life every day.

"Apart from the clipboard, anything else?" I asked. I really wanted to get into the house.

"That was the thing. A windbreaker, hat, and dark glasses. Could have been anyone," she seemed disappointed by my lack of panic. "Went around back. Let's check there first."

Us? I shrugged and went to open the side gate to the yard, Mrs. Smith's slippers less than a half step behind me.

I stopped. The gate was open. I always kept it closed for when I let Toby out. The back door to the house was open too. Wide open. I never locked it.

Toby. Where was he?

I ran up the steps to the deck and through the door into the kitchen, calling Toby's name. Mrs. Smith grabbed a rake, one that was nearly as tall as she was, and followed me into the house.

Inside, I noticed two things. First, there was no giant, 100-pound golden retriever there to greet me. Second, the big dog's bowl had been knocked over. Water was splashed all over the floor, almost as far as the landing down to the basement.

The basement.

I looked down the stairs. I could see debris on the bottom steps. Mrs. Smith saw it too. She stepped in front of me.

"I'll go first," she said, a tiny old lady with a very large new rake. "I have a weapon."

Unable to stop her, I let her pass. Down she went, the tines of the rake scraping the walls of the narrow stairwell. When she reached the bottom, Mrs. Smith, small, armed, and dangerous, turned and blocked my path down the stairs.

"Go back, Valerie. Don't come down," she ordered. "You don't want to see this. Call the RCMP."

CHAPTER FIFTEEN

This was my house. No one was keeping me from my basement. I thumped down the stairs to whatever Mrs. Smith didn't want me to see.

"I am so sorry, Valerie," she said, grabbing my arm as I moved past her. "It's my fault. Why did I wait? It wasn't Tuesday. That wasn't a meter man."

I couldn't talk.

In front of me, all I could see was destruction. Our sign-making assembly line was destroyed. Our wooden stakes were broken, our custom-made templates torn up. It looked like scene of a fight. Chairs were overturned, coffee cups spilled.

This was an attack. On me and on Darlene. In my house. This was my safe place, but it didn't feel so safe anymore.

"What's that on the wall? Writing?" Mrs. Smith asked, pointing with her rake.

I switched on the flickering overhead fluorescent lights. She was right. This wasn't spilled paint, it was a letter: X.

An X on the dark wallboard. The turquoise paint, still wet, dripped down the wall.

"X?" I asked Mrs. Smith. "What does that mean?"

We both looked at the broken signs.

"I think this means they're not going to vote for you," my neighbor said. "It sure doesn't look like it." She put down the rake and picked up the broom leaning against the wall. "They should be ashamed of themselves. Look at this mess."

I had an image of a black X on a gold ring, but I'd think about that later. Right now, I had more important things on my mind. I handed my phone to her. "Here, call 911. Where's Toby?" I was already halfway up the stairs. "I have to find my dog."

I started my search on the main floor of the house. Where was he? Had he heard something? Was he hiding? I called his name. I opened every door and every closet. There was no sign of my boy anywhere.

I yelled, "Treat!"

I checked the backyard. I looked behind the bushes where he dug and at the side where he watched for cats. I went to the front and looked up and down the street. He was nowhere in sight. I stopped everyone I met and asked them for help. I went to the playground at the school, to the next street, and to the street after that. No one had seen him. I called Darlene. I called Rollie. I hesitated but then called Stuart too.

I walked. I ran. I looked. I did everything I could to keep myself from thinking. Had the crazy person who'd trashed my basement let Toby escape, taken him, hurt him? I had to find my dog. I didn't know how.

I called the crafters. Tilly and Neil Ferguson said they'd check the trails in the woods. Annette said that she'd work the coast. Sylvie deployed her kids. I got in my car and drove down to the store, up to Darlene's house on Flying Cloud Drive, to the waterfront, to the wharf, and into the hills.

But there was no Toby.

I tried to think. If Toby had gotten out, where would he go? He was a homebody like I was. He had his chair at the store, his place next to me in my bed, and his two meals a day. That's all he wanted. Actually, no—one other thing mattered to him: me.

Toby had found me once. I knew that if he could, he would find me again.

I went home.

By the time I arrived, Officer Dawn Nolan was leaving.

"Right, the homeowner," she said, both hands on her heavy belt under the padded police vest. "You want to file a complaint?"

"Yes, I want to complain. Someone has been in my house, wrecked my basement, and destroyed useful project supplies," I said, indignant. "And my dog's gone."

Officer Nolan looked at me evenly. "Door locked?"

"Of course not."

"Okay, so no break and enter. Anything missing?"

"As far as I know, only my dog."

"Your dog was stolen?"

"The doors were open. I think he got out."

"Your dog ran away?"

"Maybe. Probably. Help me find him."

"Back to your basement. Some art supplies were messed with. And something was written on the wall."

"Yes, one letter. X. I'll clean up. But what about my dog?"

"I'll file a nuisance report. I took pictures. Looks like vandalism to me. Consider locking your doors." Nolan's face softened, if only for a minute. "About the dog, I'll contact animal control."

Her phone rang. Something on the highway. She was gone.

After we'd cleaned up, Mrs. Smith went home too. Alone, I put on a sweater and sat on the front steps. I thought of my dad. He had been a man of the woods and taught me a lot. He had a story about a hiker they found dead two hundred feet from his camp. "Don't move if you ever get lost," my dad had said. "Think of that hiker. Let them find you."

I'd do what he taught me. I'd sit in front of the house until Toby returned.

I sat, and I waited. I waited until the sun went down and the moon came out. I waited until the neighbors went to bed and the humpbacked raccoons sauntered down the street. I waited until the night-lights in the causeway disappeared and the drapes on the picture windows up and down the street were opened again. I waited through the dark, until it got even darker, and then I waited until it was light.

But no dog came home.

I tried to feel Toby out there. I strained to catch his doggy thoughts in case they were floating home with the salt breeze from the ocean. I closed my eyes. I tried to send my own hope back. *My boy, wherever you are, we'll find you,* I told him. I hoped that it was true.

I was scared.

I thought of Mike, of how I had found him. Was his killer the same person who had been in my house? Would someone like that take a dog? Would they feed him, give him water, check for ticks? What had Darlene and I gotten ourselves mixed up in? Was it my fault Toby was gone?

I couldn't wait any more. I was desperate. I would check all the same places again. I stood up. My phone beeped.

A text.

I have your dog.

CHAPTER SIXTEEN

The text was from Charlie Landry.

My fingers fumbled as I typed back.

> Where did you find him? Can I come
> and get him now?

There was a long pause. Then, an address.

I waited.

You ruined my life.

I tapped back.

> What? How?

No response.

I called Darlene.

"Charlie has Toby! I'm going to get him." My purse and my keys were already in my hand. "But something's wrong. He says I wrecked his life. Is he trying to tell me he *took* my dog?"

"Whoa. Pick me up," Darlene said. "I'm coming with you. It may be a trap."

"A trap?"

"Your basement got trashed, remember? Weird stuff on your wall? Who's the weirdest person we know? Charlie. We have to get Toby. But no way should you see him on your own."

She had a point.

"All right," I said. "Five minutes. I'm on my way."

Charlie's address was in the hills behind my house, not far from the old logging roads where Toby and I walked. If the dog had wandered up there, he would have known how to get home—unless he had been kidnapped. Would Charlie do something like that? I didn't think so. But how well did I know the man? I was glad Darlene was with me.

"Holy moly," she said when we saw the whirligigs. Dozens of them, brightly painted wooden weathervanes, lined the road to Charlie's house. "Every one's a bird."

She was right. Even though I was driving, it was hard not to be distracted. Mingled in with the usual seagulls with their rotating wings, I identified chickadees, blue jays, cardinals, woodpeckers, hummingbirds, and warblers, all carefully painted, all accurately marked. My anxiety eased a little. Surely the craftsman who had made these wouldn't harm a dog.

I heard the roosters before I saw the house.

I'd never seen a house like it. It was obvious Charlie had built the place in stages. It seemed less constructed than assembled, put together over time and without a plan, rooms added as they were needed, the doors and windows inserted whenever they could be salvaged from more coherent buildings. The end result was a structure that looked as though a bag of blocks had been tossed down from the sky. It was more a sculpture than a home.

Next to it, I saw a driveway. I started to turn into it, but Darlene stopped me with a hand on my arm.

"Don't park there. Goats." she said pointing to an old Bentley sedan parked beside the house. It looked like the ones chauffeurs drove in the movies. "Park here."

I followed her hand with my eyes. There they were, three goats on the roof of the beautiful old car, happily denting the metal with their tiny cloven hooves.

"That's goats for you," Darlene said, shaking her head. "Couldn't be serious if they tried." Darlene had been raised deeper in the country than I had. "Trust them to find the highest point and dance on it. Better park here," she said, motioning to a triangle of grass next to the mailbox, "and walk in."

When we were halfway to the house, the front door opened, and a large red-blond bullet shot out.

"Toby!" I shouted. The dog's large paws landed on my hips as he reached up to lick my face, nearly knocking me over. "You're okay!" I said, on the verge of tears. "I was so worried." Past him, I saw Charlie standing in the open doorway, a chicken in his arms, a scowl on his face.

"You've got him," he said. "Good. It's like having a pony in the house. He scared the girls," he said, holding up the hen in his arms. "Time he went home."

Darlene was not impressed. "Landry, not so fast," she said. "What was Toby doing here? Did you take him? What's this about Valerie ruining your life?" She crossed her arms. Charlie's chicken squawked. "If you're the one who was in Valerie's basement, we're calling the RCMP."

The look of belligerence on Charlie's face turned to caution.

"Come on in," he said, glaring at me. "I want to know why you did this to me. Let's do this face-to-face."

I had no idea what Charlie was talking about. I put Toby in the back of the car and followed Darlene into the maze that was the house.

Once inside, I had a closer look at the chicken. She was wearing a pink worsted sweater with a three-stranded cable down the front.

Charlie saw me staring. "Flora was a battery hen. Used up by an egg producer and left to die. All my girls are rescues," he said, motioning with his head toward the racket behind the house. "It's one of the greatest scandals of modern times. They have no feathers left by the time they come to us."

"You knit them sweaters?" Darlene asked.

"Damn right I do. It's a movement. Started in the UK. There's even a guy in Australia, 109 years old, knits for the penguins. I do my part."

I pulled myself away from the beauty of the cable, remembering why I was there. I decided to be polite to a chicken knitter. "Toby—you found him?" *Or did you take him when you broke into my house?* I wondered.

"Yes, I did. He was wandering along the road. I was going to call you, but then I read this," he pulled a paper out of a printer almost hidden behind a tower of books. "I decided to sleep on it, until I cooled down." He handed the page to us.

Landry the Liar: Darlene Disses Dirt

Our staff

Long-time community activist and candidate for mayor Charlie Landry is now known to be ineligible to run for public office. Working from a tip provided by Valerie Rankin, Darlene Mowat's campaign manager, investigative reporters have discovered that Landry, an American citizen and long-time Nova Scotia resident, has never applied for Canadian citizenship. Permanent residents like Landry have access to all Canadian services and rights but are barred from holding political office. It appears that Landry, who has run for office at the municipal and provincial levels in countless elections, has deliberately deceived voters for decades. Under provincial law, candidates are required to take an oath confirming citizenship status. Available records show that in all cases, Landry's oath was witnessed by former mayor Mike Murphy. It was not possible to reach Murphy for comment.

Front-runner candidate and well-known lawyer Brian Nickerson has asked Elections Nova Scotia not to pursue charges against Landry. "Charlie is out of the race now, and that's all that matters. But his dishonesty over the years is deeply disappointing. He owes this community an apology," says Nickerson.

I stared at the paper. I hadn't tipped anyone off. Or had I? With a sickening feeling, I remembered the message I'd left for the assignment editor. Look at the other candidates I'd said. I had had no idea it would lead to this.

Behind his smudged glasses, I could see the pain in Charlie's eyes.

"I knew I'd never be elected," he said. "But that wasn't the point. Elections give me a chance to put the habitat and wildlife on the agenda. An opportunity to speak for the silent. Protect them from development and tourism. You've taken that away from me. Why?"

From her perch in Charlie's arms, Flora stirred. Her red eyes glared at me. Who was I to hurt her dad?

Charlie bent and nuzzled her tiny, crested head. "You're upsetting my little girl," he said, narrowing his eyes at me. "I'm going to take her outside."

When Charlie was gone, Darlene and I looked around the main room. Inside, the light was dim but clear enough to see that the space was covered in books. Books in piles on the sofa and under the chairs. Books stacked under a heavy, tarnished silver tea set on the buffet, spread between unwashed plates on the kitchen table, and all over the counters. A book was even open on the stove, as though the recipe were waiting, literally, to be cooked.

When Charlie returned, Darlene came to my defense. "You had to know this would come out," she said. "Didn't you understand you weren't eligible to run?"

"Vaguely," Charlie said. "Bureaucracy's not my strong point. They asked me to swear that I was qualified to run, and I figured, 'Sure I am,' so I said yes."

"Didn't anyone check up on you?" I asked.

"Who? They didn't think that anyone would vote for me, so why bother?" Charlie stopped to think. "I think that maybe Mike knew, but he never said anything. Just a wink and a nod, like he was happy to have something on me, just in case. For a favor one day. Know what I mean?"

We did. That sounded like Mike. But it didn't make me feel any better. Politics didn't matter to me, but they mattered to Charlie. He was right. I'd taken that away from him.

I didn't know what to say. Darlene intervened. "Val wasn't out to get you," she said. "She has a big mouth. She speaks before she thinks. Everybody knows that."

I wasn't sure that *everybody* knew that but let it pass.

"Look, this is what happened," I said. "The *Lighthouse* dragged up a bunch of personal stuff about me and Darlene. I lost my cool. I asked them why they weren't doing the same to the other candidates." I took a deep breath. Charlie's living room smelled of wood smoke, grateful poultry, dry books, and damp yarn. "I never said anything about you in particular."

"You aren't the only one who's been hurt," Darlene interrupted before Charlie could respond. "Someone went into Val's basement and trashed our signs."

"They did?" Charlie asked, a flicker of interest back in his eyes. "That's political intimidation. You know what this means? They're closing in."

"Who? What are you talking about?" I asked.

"The corrupt establishment in collusion with the media." Charlie had rallied, a warrior back in business. "Crushing dissent. Same thing happening in Mexico City. Watch yourselves."

As frightening as it had been to see the mess in the house, I had a hard time imagining that the cartels had found my basement. However, Charlie had given me an idea.

"When you think of it, most of this trouble started with that stupid *Lighthouse*," I said. "The dirt they dug up, the innuendos. Someone is feeding them information about us." I thought of the paint on my wall. The X. The ring. What was the connection? "Someone so evil they will stop at nothing."

"How are you going to find out who it is?" Darlene asked. "Reporters don't reveal sources. Even I know that."

"Don't worry," I said. "I have a few media connections of my own."

CHAPTER SEVENTEEN

"Nope. No way." Noah was adamant. "If the *Lighthouse* won't name the reporter, I'm not going to."

"I just want to know who 'Our Staff' is," I said. "We're not talking about the *New York Times*. How many people are at the *Lighthouse*? You work there, you must know who it is. I want a name," I argued. "I want to straighten them out."

"Which is exactly why I can't tell you," Noah said. "I do sports now. I'm down in Lawrencetown, covering surfing. The East Coast Classic. I can't talk about this. Do you want me to lose my job?"

"Of course not." I had to go at this differently. "Answer me one question: If I wanted to draw a reporter out, what would I do?"

"That's easy," Noah said. "Find out the story they're working on. Make yourself part of it."

"I don't get it."

"It's not hard," Noah sounded distracted. I could hear a crowd cheering in the background. "Be the news."

The call ended. I looked around Charlie's kitchen. The book was off the stove, and a large, dented kettle was whistling away. Charlie and Darlene were waiting for me to say something. "He said, 'Be the news.' Does that make any sense?"

"It does," Charlie said. He put a large teapot on the table and ladled in dried leaves from a mason jar. "Tea? I foraged it myself."

Darlene and I nodded with reluctance.

"Sourdough and vegan cheese?" Charlie asked, bustling around the small kitchen. "We don't get many visitors." He dusted off a once-elegant chair with a threadbare petit-point seat. "Might have to add another room. It gets crowded, particularly in the winter."

"Why the winter?" I asked, trying to make polite conversation. I was relieved to see that my host's anger had faded.

Charlie looked surprised by my question. "I bring everyone inside. The cold is too much for the girls, not to mention the goats."

"You all live in here together? All winter?" Darlene asked, looking around. "The goats, the chickens, and that rooster? They must be big readers."

Charlie laughed. "They're only inside November to April," he explained. "I enjoy the company. Interspecies relationships are an important part of life on this planet."

True enough, I thought. Look at Toby and me. Or men and women.

"Back to the *Lighthouse* informant," Darlene reminded us. "How are we going to flush them out?"

"Relax," Charlie said. "My political instincts have been diverted but not extinguished. From now on, I'll be operating underground. I knew that day would come. I'm thinking strategy." He poured. Something that looked like moss floated to the top of the hot water in our cups. "Drink up comrades. I have a plan."

Considering that it had been thought up by a chicken sweater–knitting, moss tea–drinking, permanent-resident anarchist, it was not a bad plan. After a rehearsal, with Flora walking between the stacks of books, I was ready.

Just as I had done before, I dialed the *Lighthouse* and pressed 3. As I waited, I realized how angry I was. Darlene and I had married men who weren't who we thought they were, but how long were we supposed to pay for those mistakes? Why didn't what we had done with our lives since matter more? I wanted an answer, and I now knew how to get it.

"I have information," I began, trying to replicate the words Charlie mouthed to me across the table, "that will blow this election wide open. It's about the front-runner." I held up my palms and shrugged at my coach. Did this mean Brian? "I will share it all with you ... "—Charlie scribbled a note and passed a word over to me—"as an exclusive. On one condition." I was coming to the part we had practiced the longest. I wondered where it would lead. "I will only talk only to the reporter who wrote the story about Darlene Mowat and Valerie Rankin. I'll meet them at the back of the church parking lot." I read another note. "Eight o'clock. Behind the dumpster."

I made it to the beep. The line went dead.

"Behind the dumpster? Really? The church parking lot?" I couldn't decide whether the location for this meet-up was too dramatic or not dramatic enough.

Charlie sighed. "My apologies. Woodword and Bernstein met Deep Throat in an underground parking garage. Behind the church is the best we could do."

"Charlie and I will be close," Darlene reassured me. "You'll be safe. Talk to whoever is writing these hit pieces. Find out who is feeding them the information."

"Why would they tell me that?" I asked, still trying to get past the dumpster part of this plan. "And when they see me, won't they know it's a set-up?"

"You're there to trade," Charlie explained. "A source for a scoop. My sense is whoever the journalist is, they are ambitious. And nothing erodes ethics faster than ambition."

"They won't know who you are," Darlene added. "At least not right away. You'll be in disguise. The three-time updo champion of the Eastern Shore is going to take care of that."

"Can you make me a blond with false eyelashes?" I asked.

"That can be arranged," Darlene said.

"Then, I am in."

⌒⟨𝄔⟩⌒

Darlene was good. Even my own mother wouldn't recognize me. *I* didn't recognize me. We had borrowed the wig from Annette, and I had eyelashes on my lids the size of tiny black bathmats. Darlene had forced my feet into heels and my body into a mauve suede jacket. It was too tight for me, but Darlene said it completed "the look."

So, looking like someone else, I went behind the dumpster. The wig itched, the eyelashes pulled, and my feet hurt. I was alone and exposed. I had to remind myself that Charlie was watching from the rectory window. And Darlene was parked up the street, where she could see me in her rearview mirror. Whoever showed up, and whatever happened, I would be safe.

Eight o'clock came and went. So did eight-thirty.

I was about to give up, when I saw a tall thin figure in a hoodie scurrying along the street opposite, hugging the row of buildings like a mouse in a hallway.

I tensed. Was this the reporter? Were my negotiations about to start? What had Charlie told me to say?

My mind went blank.

Suddenly, the figure veered away from the buildings and crossed the street. I tottered out from behind the dumpster shelter. Something about this person was familiar. A hand went up, and the hood of the sweatshirt was pulled back.

I relaxed.

"Emma," I said. Tilly's granddaughter's friend. The one she had brought to a campaign meeting. The one who had made tea and passed around baked goods. "What are you doing here?"

Emma stopped, surprised.

"Excuse me?" she asked. "Do I know you?"

I remembered my disguise. I was about to explain why I was in a church parking lot, dressed up like it was Halloween, when Emma put her hand out.

"Emma Ferguson," she said. "Investigative reporter for the *Lighthouse*. I understand you have something you want to tell me?"

CHAPTER EIGHTEEN

I unbuttoned the suede jacket so I could breathe. I reached up and pulled off Annette's wig and the wig cap underneath. I shook out my own dark hair. Emma's eyes went wide. She stepped back. I looked up at the window of the rectory. Charlie's face was gone.

"It's you?" I asked, trying to process what was happening. "You're 'Our Staff'?" This was terrible. "There is no source, is there? You eavesdropped at our meetings. You used us." I tried to think of some way to express my outrage. I went mean. "You took advantage of Megan's grandmother. She is nice to you."

Emma's smooth cheeks went pink. I had touched a nerve, just as intended.

"I was just doing my job, nothing personal," she said. "You crafters talk a lot, and I listened. And I did my homework. Noah pulled some strings to get me this internship. I wanted to make the most of it. When I had something new for them every day, they noticed. This is my big chance."

"Chance for what?" I asked. I could see Charlie at the corner of the church. He was watching, waiting. "A chance to hurt people? A chance to drag out things from the past that people have a right to leave behind? To make us look like idiots? For what?"

"I hate to break it to you, Miss Rankin, but you are not the big part of this story." Emma had nerve, I gave her that. "This election is on its way to becoming a national issue. I want to be in the middle of it. It has all the ingredients. A murdered incumbent. The death of rural communities. Some candidates larger than life," she paused, "and some smaller. A senator's son using it to launch a career in national politics, maybe aim for the prime minister's office ... "

This comment got my attention. "What do you mean, 'prime minister'? Isn't this about Gasper's Cove and Drummond?"

"Oh, please." Emma looked at me with condescension. "Haven't you noticed the entourage around Nickerson? Do you really think a race in a community this size in Nova Scotia calls for the party bagmen?"

"Bagmen?" I had heard that term before. The Co-op had a few women who made fabric wallets. Duck Macdonald, our handyman at the store, made bags out of repurposed sails. How could I have forgotten that? They were such good sellers. We had a bagman.

Emma waited until she had my attention again. "The money guys, the fundraisers, the operators who make and break careers? Brian's dad brought them in for an evaluation."

"You mean for something other than this campaign?" I struggled to understand.

Emma rolled her eyes and didn't have the grace to hide it. "Honestly. The member of parliament for this area, Dunbrack, is due to retire. The party wants to keep the seat when he's gone." Emma spoke slowly to make sure that I was catching on. "They're shopping for new talent. Brian Nickerson has the connections." An image of the X-Ring flashed through my mind. "But he needs a record of public office. That's where being mayor of this new municipality comes in."

Some nonsense Brian had said between the platitudes about progress and prosperity came to me now. A vision. He had said that he had a vision for the whole country. I now knew who his real audience was.

In the distance, behind Emma, I saw Charlie making his way across the parking lot.

"Let's get this straight," I said. "We'll put aside the part about you using your host's grandmother's friends for a minute." Emma looked uncomfortable again. Grandmothers still retained their power. "Brian wants to be mayor just as a stepping-stone to bigger and better things. Am I right?"

Emma crossed her arms in front of her University of King's College sweatshirt and nodded.

"Mike's death was awfully convenient for him, wasn't it?" I asked her. "Off the record."

As soon as the words were out of my mouth, I knew that I had gone too far. *Rankin Rats Out Killer* flashed across my mind. I had to find a way to backtrack, and quickly.

"Look," I said to Emma. "Don't quote me on that." I could tell by her face the young reporter was planning on doing just that. What did I have to bargain with?

"Maybe we can work together," I suggested. Emma looked skeptical. "I'm already sort of working on a murder case with the RCMP, in a consulting capacity," I continued.

"I wasn't implying that Brian was a suspect in this investigation," I said with an authority I did not have. If Wade heard any of this, the next dead body would be mine. "Any more than any number of people we are considering."

I was getting in deeper and deeper but couldn't stop now. Charlie had joined us, but Emma ignored him. I had her full attention. I gave Charlie a sideways glare from under my false eyelashes.

"If you keep that little comment to yourself, for obvious reasons, because this is an ongoing investigation," I added, silently thanking Netflix for my legal education, "in return, I promise to be your confidential source from the inside. No one but you, and Charlie, I guess, know about this." With regret, I resisted the impulse to say that if she told anyone, I would have to kill her. Such a good line.

Emma made a quick mental calculation. We were two people with no information trying to do a trade of nothing at the back of a church parking lot. Next to a dumpster.

"Deal," she said finally. "With limits. If any other news outlet finds out something about this murder investigation before I do, all bets are off. You got that?"

Something about Emma Ferguson's tone made me want to tell her to go clean her room, but I held back. I pretended that we were equals, something neither of us believed.

"Deal," I agreed. "You'll be hearing from me."

Emma stared at me for a minute and then put up her hood, turned back to the street, and walked away.

When she was out of earshot, Charlie looked at me.

"Did you dig yourself a deep enough hole on that one?" he asked. "Since when are you working with the RCMP? I am sure that would be news to them."

"A bit of an exaggeration," I said. "Wade asked me to let him know if I ran across anything. He probably said the same to a lot of people."

Charlie grunted. "Not to me. But if overstating your position within law enforcement got that journalist hack off your back, it was worth it." He stopped to pick up some trash from the gravel of the lot and put it into the dumpster. "Also, you made a good point. It looks like Brian Nickerson just might have the best motive of anyone for Mike's murder."

CHAPTER NINETEEN

I couldn't sleep that night.

I tried.

I had been up most of the night before. I was tired. But whenever I closed my eyes, I had an image of a giant seam ripper called "politics" coming down out of the sky to rip open the comfortable cushion of my life in Gasper's Cove. I saw all the parts of the past Darlene and I had pushed down deep, pulled out like stuffing. I saw Mighty Mike Murphy dead on a shabby rug under his desk. I saw the inside of an election campaign and how it changed people. How it had turned a granddaughter's friend into a mean reporter. How it had transformed a harmless bureaucrat into an egomaniac. And how it had taken the two calm masts of my life, Rollie and Stuart, away from me, abandoned over a ring and a club that would not let me in.

But worst of all, the conflict of this election had started to change who I was. I wasn't sure whether I was as nice anymore. What was I doing arguing with friends and family over signs? Why was I leaving angry messages on phones, causing trouble for other people?

Somewhere in the night, out in the dark woods, I heard an owl. What had Charlie said? A voice for the voiceless. He wanted to take care of the plovers, just like Darlene wanted to protect the town.

Was this campaign the best way to do it?

With that question unanswered, alone with my dog, I finally fell asleep.

⌒⟀⌒

As soon as I opened my eyes the next morning, it hit me. Today was Friday.

Gilles was coming for dinner at 6:00.

My sleep deficit no longer mattered. I had a dog to walk, a store to run, a house to clean, and, according to Darlene's instructions, makeup to apply.

I skated through the day with one eye on my watch. Business was light. At 3:00, Colleen shooed me out the front door. At 3:23, I sped-walked Toby. At 3:52, I located the vacuum. At 4:11, I emptied the dishwasher and ran around the house with a spray bottle and sponge. At 4:47, I exited my pink and gray bathroom, ready for the evening.

I had passable eyeliner on at least one eye. I had a bun on the top of my head, and it was definitely messy. My cleavage was hoisted, and my shoes were flat. I'd done what I could do.

I stopped to catch my breath and tried to assemble my thoughts. It had been a long time since I'd had a male over. I tried to remember. What if he flirted? What if he didn't? Could a man know how long it had been?

The doorbell rang.

I wasn't ready. I never would be.

I opened the door and smelled his cologne. I'd forgotten to put on perfume. It didn't matter now.

Gilles's hair was damp from his shower. His shirt was pressed, and the sleeves were rolled up to expose his muscular forearms. He had a large bag of groceries in one hand, two bottles of wine and a bouquet of calla lilies in the other.

He reached over and kissed me, first on one cheek, then the other. He handed me the flowers, walked into the kitchen, and put his bag on the counter. From down the hallway, Toby watched him, lifted his nose to assess the cologne, and marched off down the hall.

Gilles wasted no time getting to work. He moved around the kitchen like he already knew it. He uncorked both bottles of wine and set them next to the kitchen sink to breathe. Efficiently, he unpacked a roll of parchment paper, tomatoes, salad greens, lemon, onion, garlic, bundles of herbs, and wild rice. He laid them next to a tightly wrapped pink parcel from the butcher. This meal was going to be more complicated than the ham and scalloped potatoes I usually served company.

"I'm impressed," I said. "What are we having? Can I help?"

"No, no, all under control," Gilles said. "Nothing too complex. *Veau en papillote.* I hope you like it."

I translated. Veal in paper? Not a Gasper's Cove standard.

"One of my favorites," I lied. "Thank you."

Gilles poured us each a glass of wine. He found my cutting board, sharpened one of my knives, and started to chop. I sat back and watched. It was like a cooking show. The veal was searing in the pan when the front doorbell rang. With my wine glass in my hand, I went to the door. *Please don't let this be one of the crafters tonight. If they see this, they will want to stay*, I thought.

I pulled the door open. It wasn't a crafter.

Stuart was on my front step.

"Oh, hi," he said, looking past me to the kitchen, taking it all in. "I didn't know you had company." Awkwardly, he lifted a ziplock bag. "I wanted to drop these off. I felt bad how we left things the other day. This is sort of a peace offering."

Gilles came up behind me and, with one hand on my shoulder, reached over and took the bag from Stuart.

"Ah, excellent," he said. "Muffins?" He opened the bag and sniffed. "Blueberry?" I saw an index card with Stuart's neat engineering printing in the bag—the recipe. Stuart never forgot the details.

"Rhubarb," Stuart said. "From my garden, and bran." He looked like he wanted to go home.

Gilles raised an eyebrow. "Bran? How thoughtful. You certainly seem like a regular kind of guy. Come in, can we offer you a glass of wine?"

Stuart ignored the offer but took a few steps forward. He gestured to the parchment paper and scissors on the kitchen table. "Making paper dolls?" he asked.

Gilles laughed. The sheet of parchment had been creased in half and trimmed at both ends. Gilles unfolded the paper. He held up a giant heart, like an outsized beige Valentine. "For the veal," he explained, folding the paper over again. "It's traditional. The meat goes at the top, and the juices gather at the bottom. Quite romantic, don't you think?" he said, winking at Stuart.

"I wouldn't know." Stuart put his fists in the pockets of his jeans, as he stood in the doorway. "I'm more of a BBQ and steak man myself," he said, walking back to the front entry. "I've got to go. To the office. I'm designing a bridge. Four lanes. It's a big project."

Gilles smiled. "Nice local fellow," he said after Stuart left.

Dinner, more elegant than any my aunt's dining table had seen before, was spectacular. Gilles was finished long before I was. That's because I talked. And talked. I wasn't sure whether it was the company or the wine I found more intoxicating. This man was a good listener. He let me speak and nodded with sympathy as I went on and on. It was so easy to tell him about a marriage where I was happy and the other person was not. He understood when I told him how when my children went away, I felt that I had failed again. He heard me when I explained why I came home to Gasper's, about the Co-op, about my plans for the future, the craft retreats, and online sales.

"These crafters, you work a lot together?" he asked when I finally wound down. "Like this election, you organize them, you're the leader?"

"I guess you could say that," I said, flattered. "That's why I felt so bad when all the work they did got smashed up in the basement."

"Smashed? Vandalism? Why didn't I know about this?" Gilles seemed annoyed.

Then, I remembered. He was in public relations but still with the RCMP. Should Dawn Nolan have told him what had happened downstairs?

"It was upsetting, but not a lot of damage was done. We cleaned it up," I explained. I hoped that Dawn wouldn't get into trouble. "We make our signs in my basement. Someone came in and smashed a few up. Your people came out. They think it was kids."

"Kids? Who thought that up? Where did they break in? How?" Gilles got up from the table and tossed his napkin down. "Come. Show me."

Why was he so upset? "Okay, follow me," I said, leading Gilles through the kitchen to the stairs.

Once we were in the basement, I showed Gilles all I could. "They broke about seven signs." I pointed to a wall. "And they painted an X over there. We washed it off. It was water-soluble paint."

Gilles stopped his patrol around the windows and looked at me. "An X?" he asked. "Are you sure?"

"Didn't make sense to me either," I said.

Gilles returned to his inspection. "Show me the point of entry. Where they came in."

"Point of entry?" I asked. "The back door? It wasn't locked."

"Not locked?" Gilles shook his head. "Let me guess. The front door was unlocked too."

"I don't even know where my house key is," I said. "If I locked the door, how would anyone, like my relatives, get in?"

"That's the point of keys," Gilles said, "in the rest of the world."

I looked away so my guest wouldn't see me biting my tongue. Maybe it was late. I had dishes to wash ...

"I'm sorry," Gilles said, touching my face. "This is ... it's unsettling. I don't understand, or maybe I do, why you are minimizing this. You need to be more careful. Do you know what I am saying?"

Overhead, I could hear Toby's nails on the hardwood hallway. His end-of-the-day walk was long overdue.

"Thank you for a wonderful meal," I said. I was flustered by the attention and concern. "But don't worry about me. You would be surprised at how careful I am."

Gilles smiled. "Actually, nothing you do would surprise me. That's what interests me."

I felt like I was twenty.

Upstairs, I heard the rattle of a dog leash dragged across the floor. It was a sound that was impossible to ignore. "I'm sorry," I said, reluctantly. "I have a dog to walk."

"No problem," Gilles said, smoothing my hair with his hand and looking across the basement to the door that led to the backyard. "You go up and take care of the dog. I'll let myself out down here."

I heard the door close behind him.

CHAPTER TWENTY

The sound of my front door opening woke me. The guard dog on my bed snored.

Someone was in the kitchen.

I reached for my housecoat and slippers. I'd told Gilles that I was careful. It was time to pretend that I was. Water ran in the sink. A cupboard door opened. Someone was making coffee.

I tiptoed down the hallway.

Darlene.

I should have known.

"Oh, hi," she said. "Hope I didn't wake you. I couldn't wait. I came over for the details."

"Details?"

Darlene raised her eyebrows and looked at the counter. She would never have gone to bed without every last dish done.

"Your romantic dinner with your private chef. How did it go?" she asked.

The coffee machine gurgled. There was a thump down in the bedroom as four golden retriever paws hit the floor.

"Good. Nice. Great food," I said. I left out the parchment paper heart, the two bottles of wine, and a middle-aged sewing teacher who couldn't shut up.

"And?" Darlene hadn't come to hear about food. "How late did he stay?" She caught herself and looked down the hall. "He's not still here, is he?"

"Darlene! You know me. Of course not," I said. "Gilles was very nice. But you'll laugh at this—Stuart showed up. With muffins."

"Get out!" Darlene stopped massaging her neck to stare at me. "How did that go?"

"He didn't stay long." I changed the subject. "I've got to get that wig back to Annette, don't I?"

"Would you mind?" Darlene asked. "Listen, while I'm here, do you have any calamine?"

"In the medicine cabinet. Why?"

Darlene pulled down the neckline of her knit top. "I've got these weird hives. They won't go away."

I put my hands on my cousin's shoulders and moved her closer to the light of the window. These weren't hives. Darlene's neck and upper chest were marked with a rash, almost blisters.

"Oh my," I said. "I don't like the look of this. Why haven't you seen a doctor? Does it hurt?"

"I showed it to Dr. Clarke yesterday afternoon. He told me to check the cats for fleas." Darlene rearranged her top.

I rolled my eyes. Dr. Clarke, over in Drummond, was at least 98 years old. No one but Darlene's family went to him.

He was a widower and had been married to one of the old aunts. They didn't want to hurt his feelings.

"Maybe you should see someone else," I suggested. "Stuff like that could get infected." I poured myself a coffee and then made up my mind. "Get in the car, we're going over to the hospital. You need to see someone who knows what they're doing."

───

We were in luck when we arrived in the ER. The triage nurse on duty was one of my sewing students. She rushed us through and put us in an examining room.

We didn't wait long.

At first, the doctor didn't say much. She said "Hmm," pulled down Darlene's shirt, examined the affected area, said "Hmm" a few more times, and then stood back.

"First, these are not flea bites. Not ticks either, thank goodness," she said. Ticks and the Lyme disease they carried moved farther north every year. "That's the good news. No, this looks like contact dermatitis from something caustic. Any idea of what that could be?"

"You mean an acid, like a chemical?" I asked.

"Exactly," the doctor said. "Cleaning fluids, ammonia, or oven cleaner?"

"Nothing I haven't used for years," Darlene said. "I have redhead skin. I'm careful what I use, and I clean all the time." It was true. Darlene, like her mother, went through life with a sponge in her hand.

The doctor thought. "What about cosmetics? Anything new?"

Darlene and I glanced at each other and closed ranks. We'd had the same thought. Maybe "Buy Local" wasn't such a good idea. How much had we sold? What were our best sellers?

"Possibly," Darlene said. "I'll think about it. I'll check at home."

The doctor studied us as though she had another question to ask. She sighed, picked up Darlene's chart, and wrote on it. "Do that," she said. "And if things don't clear up, come back and see us."

⌒⅄⌒

Sylvie Kylberg sat at her kitchen table, arms crossed, angry and indignant. When I arrived, she had been in the middle of weaving placemats out of recycled dog leashes. It was not going well. As hard as she tried, even when she hammered the joints down with a can of tomatoes, the nylon strapping would not lay flat. No one was going to buy placements that made your drinks fall over.

That was not the only reason she was upset. I had just suggested that her handmade face creams might be giving customers second-degree burns.

"Are you saying I am hurting people with my cosmetics?" she asked, voice shrill. "I'm running a Health Canada–inspected crack operation here, everything to regulation."

I looked around her kitchen/production facility. Her tabby cat stalked by me on the counter, tail high, nose up in the air. He calmly sat down on a cream cheese–iced carrot cake.

"I can see that," I said. I knew the ingredients she listed on her creams: sea kelp, shea butter, and love. "But is it possible—it's only an idea—that someone could have tampered with your product?" *Like that cat there on the cake*, I wanted to say.

"No way. Look," Sylvie held up a tiny jar so I could see the tape wrapped around it. "Tamper-proof. They'd have to break the seal. Remember what happened to Johnson & Johnson with Tylenol in 1982? I have childproof packaging." One of her dark curls was stuck to her forehead with icing. She handed me a jar. "Get it analyzed!"

I was afraid that she'd suggest that. How did that work? I knew how to order interfacing but not lab tests. Could I ask Wade who did his dog-hair analysis? No, that might be a sensitive topic. The cat was up on the windowsill, licking his paw. I had a better idea.

"How's this?" I asked. "I'll hold your cream aside until we get it tested, for the customers' sake." No need to tell her that I had already asked Colleen to move the jars into my office. "Not that I think there's a problem," I added. The cat jumped off the counter and chased a craft pom-pom across the floor.

Sylvie was not taken in by my diplomacy. She stood up, opened a drawer, and pulled out a table knife.

"How's this?" she asked, smoothing over the slightly hairy dent in the side of her cake. "I quit the campaign team until I get an apology. Maybe I'll even vote for somebody else." She stopped to lick icing off the knife. "You can't just go around making accusations. One day that's going to get you into big trouble. Maybe today's that day."

CHAPTER TWENTY-ONE

I left Sylvie putting birthday candles on the cake. She'd grunted when I said goodbye. I knew that I'd hurt her feelings, but the sooner I got to the bottom of Darlene's mysterious rash, the better for everyone. Better for Darlene's neck, better for the Co-op's reputation, and better for Sylvie's future in seaweed cosmetics.

What I needed right now was help. Who did I know who was scientific, not creative? Precise, not artistic? My mind was blank. Then, I remembered some productive gossip. I called Darlene and told her my plan.

Kenny MacQuarrie, the local building inspector, lived next to Annette. Once, Darlene had seen them together at the Peking Palace. Twice, I'd spotted them at the Agapi. Three times this month, he'd picked her up after sewing classes.

Kenny knew testing. Annette knew Kenny. Maybe he would know what to do about Sylvie's cream.

Plus, if the inspector couldn't help me, a trip out to Hirtle Avenue was never wasted. The view from the short street over the ocean was spectacular. Seeing the water would calm me. I needed that.

The street was really a lane, a row of three houses built when the Hirtle family sold the land. Annette lived in the middle bungalow, a couple from away on one side, and Kenny and his bulldog, Max, on the other.

As I turned onto the street, I saw Kenny and Annette in her front yard. They were side by side in wooden Adirondack chairs, one pink and one yellow, facing the ocean. The two chairs were pushed together so a plate of oatcakes could balance on the armrests. Max stretched out at their feet, snoring and content.

When he saw me, Kenny jumped up and pulled another chair, a turquoise one, next to his.

I handed Annette the bag with the wig in it.

"Thank you," she said. "I hope it was what you needed." She opened the top of the bag and showed it to Kenny.

"Ah, Roca Margarita Blonde," he said peering down at the wig. "One of my favorites." He looked at Annette, a brunette today, and giggled. She giggled back. They looked like two middle-aged people in Grade 7. I waited for the giggling to stop, then plowed on with my mission.

"Kenny, I have a technical question," I said. "I wonder if you can help me out."

At the word *technical*, Kenny's head snapped up. He sat up straighter in his chair, or at least as straight as the slope of the Adirondack would allow, and pushed his aviator glasses farther up his short nose.

"If I can, I will. We both will," he said looking at Annette, who nodded. "What's going on?"

"I've been at the ER with Darlene—nothing serious, but she has a strange rash on her neck," I said. "The doctor said it was contact dermatitis. A burn of some kind." I took Sylvie's jar of face cream out of my purse and handed it to Kenny. "I wonder, is there any way we could find out if this caused that reaction?"

At first, Kenny didn't say anything. Then, taking one of Annette's cloth napkins, he carefully unscrewed the jar's top and sniffed the contents.

"I don't smell much. Seaweed, maybe shoe polish. You said the doctor told you it looked like a chemical burn?" he asked.

"That's exactly what she said." As I talked, I realized how crazy this sounded.

"What do you think, Ken? Anything you can do?" Annette asked.

"A proper toxicology analysis would have to be done in Halifax. But if you're just testing for a corrosive, I can do that, I suppose. The key measure is the pH level. I have kits in the house. We use them for well water."

"Could you check it out?" I asked. "As a favor?"

Kenny chose his words carefully. "I can tell you if the acid level is below neutral, which would mean too much, or if the base level is above, for alkaline. If either of those levels is off, what's in here might burn." He waved the small jar under suspicion. "I could tell you that much."

"Ken, can you test it now?" Annette asked. "Valerie needs help. We'll drink tea while you do it." I had a glimpse of their relationship. Annette had the confidence that came with security.

Kenny was up and out of his chair immediately. Annette and I watched as he and Max marched off to the house next door as instructed.

Alone with Annette, I couldn't resist. "He's a nice guy," I said, searching for something else flattering to say about the dour city official who had nearly prevented me from opening the Co-op over some building regulations. "You seem to get along well." If there was a real romance here, Darlene would want to know.

I wasn't fooling Annette.

She looked out at the water, a small smile on her face. "You know, when I married Darrell, I thought I had snagged the hottest guy in town," she laughed. "Look at how that turned out." She glanced at me. "Sometimes what you are looking for doesn't look the way you expected."

Out of nowhere, I had an image of Gilles's Citroën. I pulled myself back to the present.

"Darlene still wants to run you know, despite everything that's happened," I said. I was desperate to talk about something else. "Charlie is out. That leaves Elliot and Brian. They seem to know what they're doing. We don't."

Annette snorted. "I can't talk about Brian—he doesn't come to my Tupperware parties. But Elliot, that's another story." She leaned closer to me and looked around. "Ken got involved with Charlie because of the bird nests. He's heard a few things about the other campaigns, and he knows Elliot from work. He'd kill me for repeating this, but he says Elliot has no choice but to run now that Mike is gone. He says it's his only hope for a job."

"What do you mean?" I asked, picking up an oatcake. "He's the deputy mayor."

"*Was* deputy mayor, before this election," Annette corrected. "He got that position because Mike appointed him, but Mike was slipping in the polls." She picked up a teapot from a little table and poured me a cup. "Elliot's only the head of the Gasper's Cove division of the department. With amalgamation, chances are he'll be demoted, or even out of a job." She paused to give me a look over her mug. "Unless he was the mayor himself. That would change things, be a step up."

"How would he be elected?" I asked. "Do people know Elliot enough to vote for him?"

"It doesn't matter," Annette said, looking me straight in the eye. "You know this community as well as I do. Loyalties are strong, particularly if you've passed away. Everyone can pretend they always liked you. Mike is more popular dead than alive. His endorsement, the sympathy vote, could get his deputy elected ... "

"Elliot's campaign is based on a murder?" I asked. My mind was whirling.

"I'd say so," Annette answered. *"This one's for Mike."*

We heard Kenny's front door open. He and Max bobbed down the stairs and walked over to us. Kenny handed me the jar.

"Nothing unusual," he said. "The pH is balanced. I can't see anything to cause a corrosive burn."

"The cream is out?" I asked. Sylvie was vindicated. I looked like a fool.

Kenny chose his words carefully. "All I can say is that there is nothing caustic in this jar." He paused to think. "How about skin allergies? Did you consider that?"

No, we hadn't. The first thing I'd thought was the most dramatic.

"I'll check that out," I said. "I appreciate it."

I waited until I was back in the car to call Darlene. She didn't even say "Hello" when she answered.

"And? Was Kenny any help?" she asked.

"Sort of," I answered. "He doesn't think the cream could have burned your skin, but he had a good question."

"What's that?"

"Allergies. You don't have any allergies, do you?" I asked. "Something I don't know about?"

"No. No one in my family is allergic to anything. We grew up in the woods," she reminded me. "Dr. Clarke says that dirt's good for kids. Toughens them up."

How did the Mayo Clinic manage without Dr. Clarke?

"Nothing else?"

"Positive. I burn in the sun, and the only thing I am allergic to is beige fabric. Takes the color right out of my face," Darlene said.

"Don't think that counts as an allergy," I told her. "I have to apologize to Sylvie. I guess you can start using that cream again."

"I can't. I threw it out," Darlene said. "I'm glad I didn't pay for it. I brought home the tester. Kind of gummy, and the seaweed wasn't mixed in real well."

An alarm went off in my head. "The tester?"

"Yes. Mom and I opened a jar for people to try. No one would go near it. So, I brought it home," Darlene added, as if this made some sense.

"Why?"

"It was Polly's idea. She says celebrity endorsement moves product," Darlene continued. "I'm always in the news, we both are. She thinks I have a future as an influencer. Do you know what that is?"

I didn't but let it pass. I could hardly process everything I had in my brain. An open jar at the store. I was back at square one.

"Both in the news?" I asked, distracted. I'd thought that Emma was going to back off.

"Your basement's the big story," she said. "There's other stuff, don't pay any attention. But Brian's still talking about that deputy mayor thing. I thought you'd straightened that out."

"I had. I did." I was indignant. "I practically threw Stuart out of the store when he suggested it. You know that."

"Well, you better track him down and tell him again," Darlene said. "I don't think Brian got the message."

As soon as Darlene hung up, I went to the *Lighthouse*'s website. It was worse than I'd expected.

Catty Candidate Calling It Quits?

Underground HQ Trashed as Supporters Walk Away

Sources say that long-shot candidate Darlene Mowat's troubled campaign for mayor may be drawing to a close. They are laying the blame at the feet of her campaign manager, Valerie Rankin.

Rankin's tactics have come into question since the withdrawal of popular local fixture, Charlie Landry, from the race.

"Charlie wasn't hurting nobody. Not like anyone voted for him," says Gasper's Cove entrepreneur Harry Sutherland. "We all got something in our history. It was a dirty trick to drag out his past, especially now."

Rumors have circulated for some time that volunteers are uncomfortable with Rankin's influence. A recent visit by this reporter to the election office Rankin runs in her residence found it deserted and the campaign materials destroyed. Sylvie Kulberg, until recently a Mowat for Mayor volunteer, has said in an email that she now supports Brian Nickerson.

When asked to comment, Nickerson's response was conciliatory. "It's important not to judge Miss Mowat by the actions of one member of her staff. Darlene was a popular councillor during her tenure on the Gasper's Cove council. She can still contribute, in the appropriate role. That's why we are in negotiations right now to have her join a Nickerson administration as deputy mayor."

The Lighthouse has been unable to reach Rankin for comment. An employee at her place of business says that she believes that Rankin is on a drive along the coast, with no estimated time of return.

I was stunned. That was fast. Sylvie must have contacted the *Lighthouse* as soon as I left. I felt sick. I wanted to weep, but the tears wouldn't come. I was too mad. I'd come home to Gasper's Cove for peace, quiet, and stability. Where had that gone? How did I get from my sewing room to here? This was not my world. What was it about politics that brought out the worst in everyone, even me? Why would anyone want this?

I didn't. I called the store.

"Colleen? Do you think you'd be all right on your own the rest of the day?" I asked.

"We'll be fine," she said, then hesitated. She'd heard the crack in my voice. "I thought you were out at Hirtle Avenue. Everything okay?"

"Toby needs to get out," I said. "And I need a breather."

"You deserve it," Colleen said. "Take care of yourself, my dear."

Colleen's tone touched me, but I still couldn't cry. Feeling sorry for myself wouldn't get me anywhere. This had to stop. I remembered the last line in that awful article: "a drive along the coast." That's what I'd do. Toby and I would head out, and we wouldn't come back until we had this all figured out.

CHAPTER TWENTY-TWO

Toby and I took the long way out of town to the north shore of the island. I was in no hurry to get where I wanted to go because I didn't know where I was going.

I also didn't know what to think.

Too much had happened, most of it bad. I drove past the turn-off to Charlie's house. I thought of the trouble I'd brought him. I passed the Bluenose Inn. Was I still welcome there? I turned up the hill and looked down at the yacht club on the water. Was a little part of me like Elliot Carter? Were we both struggling to get the respect we craved?

I didn't have the answers. I kept driving through the spruce trees until the road opened again onto a view of the sea. To my left was a row of tiny fishermen's cottages. I saw the one where Tilly and Neil Ferguson lived, next to one owned by Trevor Ross, the art teacher. Farther along, these small homes gave way to big houses built by those who had made their money in places more prosperous, but not as pretty, as Gasper's Cove. I looked out onto the point and saw two flags high up on tall poles, one red and white, the

Canadian flag, the other white with the blue cross of Nova Scotia. The flags flew between two houses with the best views on the island. This estate was the Nickerson summer compound, one house for Will, and one for his father. The Nickersons understood this game that Darlene and I were no good at. People like them made the rules.

Toby and I went on, farther and farther, away from the development to the land as it was before. When we had driven far enough, I pulled over and parked on the shoulder. I opened the door and let Toby jump out. There was no need for a leash here. I let him run down to the beach, and I followed. A large log had drifted in from the ocean. I sat on it and watched Toby zigzag after the seagulls.

I began to relax. I knew why.

My dad used to take me to this place when I was little. That's why I was here. Here, where traces of my father, who knew so much, still were.

I wished that I could hear his voice now.

In my childhood, my father and I would walk on this beach and then go behind into the hills. My dad loved those times as much as I did. He was a scientist. He believed that children should know where they lived and what was around them. My dad taught me the difference between the footprints of a deer and a coyote, between the berries and mushrooms I could eat and those I couldn't. He used the Latin names for most of the plants, and when I couldn't remember them, he translated. There was one I thought of now, with a funny name. A big, tall plant, a larger version of what grew on the lawn. He took it very seriously. What was it?

Then, I remembered. The Giant Hogweed.
Of course.

When we were back in cell phone range, I stopped and made my call to the biology division of the Nova Scotia Department of Natural Resources, my dad's old office.

"Does a Rob Baxter still work with you?" I asked the receptionist.

"Yes, he does. Part-time these days," she answered. "You're in luck. He's in the office now. Would you like me to put you through?"

"Yes, please." Rob had been my dad's assistant just before he retired. When he came on the line, I caught my breath. Hearing his voice brought back memories.

"Valerie Rankin. I don't believe it! We were just talking about your dad the other day," Rob said. "How are you? I hear you're back in Gasper's Cove."

"I am." I was unsure of how to begin this conversation. "Listen, Rob, I hate to hit you out of the blue like this, but I have a question about a plant my dad talked about a long time ago. I have a friend, someone running for mayor up here, who might have run into it. Not poison ivy, but similar."

I thought that I could hear Rob smile. He was a man who waited all day for calls like mine.

"If I can help you, I will," he said. "But what plant are we talking about?"

"Giant Hogweed," I said. I felt like a character out of *Harry Potter.*

"You think that your friend had an encounter with a Giant Hogweed?" Rob sounded alarmed. "I hope not. The small garden variety is benign, but the larger version, the six-foot plant we have in parts of the province, is dangerous. Where was this?"

Possibly in a jar of face cream made with seaweed and love, I could have said, but didn't. "Not sure exactly."

"Find out if you can." I could hear the tapping of keys— Rob was taking notes. "We've got a public information campaign going on in your neck of the woods. The sap is photosensitive. If it gets in your eyes, it can cause blindness. Nothing to fool around with."

Wow. If this plant had caused Darlene's rash, she was lucky. I had another question, an important one.

"What if someone didn't touch the sap directly? Say it was more of a secondhand contact." My dad's old colleague must think that I was nuts. "Would it be as dangerous?" I asked.

There was silence as Rob thought. "You mean like some sap left on a glove or a tool? And it got touched later with a bare hand?" Rob, bless him, wasn't considering the cosmetic angle, only scenarios that made sense in his sane world.

"Sort of like that."

"Okay. It would still burn, but not as much," he said. "Can't say I've seen any research on that scenario. I imagine if the sap hadn't dried up, it could still do some damage. But, like I said, it's photosensitive. It would be most active as soon as the person went out in the sun."

I was glad I had made this call. "That's interesting," I said. "Really appreciate this."

"Any time," he answered. "Remember, if you get a location on the plant, let us know. We'll send up a crew to remove it."

"If I can figure that out, I will."

"Someone running for mayor, did you say?" Rob asked. "Can I ask who? It wouldn't be Elliot Carter, though, that's for sure."

That caught me by surprise. "Why not Elliot?" I asked.

"Oh, we all know Elliot, he kicked around a lot," Rob explained. "One of the departments he worked in was Land and Forests. He'd know better than to mess with the Giant Hogweed."

"No, it wasn't Elliot," I said, thinking that this unexpected piece of information was exactly what I needed. "Someone else, kind of confidential."

"Got it. Politicians." Rob stopped. When he spoke again, he was less official, more wistful. "I'm glad you called. We still miss Ed Rankin—he was the best. Always did the right thing. You sound just like him."

"Thanks, Rob," I said. "I needed to hear that. You take care."

After I hung up, I didn't go back onto the road right away. Instead, I sat and stared at the horizon on the water. Toby sat patiently beside me, willing to wait for as long as I needed.

I knew what I had to do. After I dropped Toby off at home, I got back in the car and headed across the causeway to the RCMP detachment in Drummond.

It was time I talked to Wade.

CHAPTER TWENTY-THREE

As I was coming off the causeway, I passed Gilles's Citroën going in the other direction, heading over to Gasper's Cove. Gilles saw me and flashed his lights. I smiled as we passed, aware of the flutter I felt.

I'd pulled myself together by the time I arrived at the detachment. The officer at the front desk was the one I knew.

"Is Officer Corkum in?" I asked her. "I have something to tell him."

"I'll buzz him," she said, watching me through the plexiglass window as she mumbled something into her phone, listened, and then hung up. "He'll be out shortly. Why don't you take a seat?"

I didn't sit down. This seemed like an opportunity to talk. I never let those pass.

"Good news about that award they're giving Wade. When's that going to happen?" I asked, kicking the conversational tires. "I passed that public relations guy on the way over." Gilles had been in the area for a while. I wondered whether he was good at this job or just slow at it.

"Award? You know as much as I do," she said.

I tried again, hoping that the officer wouldn't wonder why I was so interested in an RCMP staffer from Québec.

"You're from Isle Madame, aren't you?" I asked. "So was his grandfather. I think that's one reason he came."

"Excuse me?" the officer asked. "What gave you that idea?"

Because that's what he told me, I wanted to say. "His grandfather went to Québec to work in the mills?" I ventured.

The face behind the plexiglass looked puzzled. "You got that wrong. I know everyone from the island and their fathers," she said. "But my mother is a DeWolf. When I heard the name, I asked him about his family. He said that his people originally came from Connecticut."

Before I could say anything, a door down the corridor opened. Wade came out.

"Well, look who's here," he said. "You wanted to talk to me?" He moved me out of earshot from the front desk and to an empty room, not his office.

"Yes. I've been doing some work on the case. Mike's murder, like you asked," I said. "I want to report on the progress of my investigations." I sat down and settled in, realizing how much I enjoyed being here in a semiofficial capacity.

Wade pulled up another one of the molded plastic chairs and sat. He moved uncomfortably in his seat and looked at a spot on the wall behind my head. I was surprised by his lack of enthusiasm.

"I didn't ask you to *investigate*," he said. "I just asked you to let me know if you noticed anything. I hope you haven't been talking."

Wade couldn't have it both ways. He couldn't ask me to help one day and then not listen to me the next. "Hear me out," I said.

"All right, but understand there is more at stake than you know." Wade leaned back and locked his hands behind his head, as if to show me that he wasn't going to take anything I said seriously.

"Mike was murdered"—I paused dramatically, I couldn't resist—"by the same person who is trying to make Darlene look bad."

Wade tipped so far back in his chair that I thought that he might fall over. He caught himself and sat up straight.

"This is my fault. I should never have involved you," he said. "I'm under real pressure on this case." Wade put a finger under his collar to loosen it. "I don't have time for this. You've figured this out? Give me a break."

It had taken nerve to come here. I wasn't leaving until I had said what I came here to say. Wade needed to pay attention to me.

"Think about it." This was a mistake. Wade the jock had always been sensitive about his intellect. "The murderer is out to get Darlene. That shows you who it is," I explained.

"Not following," Wade said, then caught himself. "I mean, I can follow. It just doesn't make sense."

"Darlene," I said. "There's a target on her back. A sign with her name is put next to a dead body. Personal stuff about her finances is leaked to the media. Her campaign manager—that would be me—is dragged through the dirt. Her headquarters down in my basement is ransacked. And now her skin is all broken out due to sabotage. Who would go to all that trouble?"

"You tell me," Wade said.

"Someone who wants to be mayor of an enlarged municipality. Something no candidate but Darlene opposes. One of the other candidates, the same one who killed Mike." If I was going to do all of Wade's work for him, he owed me a commission. "Elliot Carter."

"Elliot?" Wade rolled his eyes. "And what's your evidence?"

"Money and ego," I explained. "Elliot is addicted to job titles. Being mayor gives him everything he needs. Mike stood in his way."

Wade looked out the window, but I could tell that he was listening. I could almost hear the rusty wheels turning in his head. Maybe something I said had connected to something he already knew.

"Go on."

"Elliot used to work at Lands and Forests. And he is in the store all the time," I said. "It could have been him."

"Now you've lost me again," said Wade.

I might as well go all the way. "At first, I thought it was Charlie," I explained. "He can't stand the tourists who come here. They walk on protected lichen; they knock over bird's nests. I thought he gave himself away, serving us moss tea, telling us he was a forager. Then, I remembered the chicken sweaters. Character counts."

Wade picked up a pen and started clicking it. "I don't believe this," he said. "Today of all days. What are you talking about?"

"Giant Hogweed sap," I said. "I think Elliot put some of it in the tester for Sylvie's antiaging cream." I found the clicking distracting. "I'm sure he thought no one would figure it out. But I did. It was plain as anything."

Wade was now doodling. Tight little circles, like spirals. I wasn't sure whether he understood what I was saying.

"That sap," I explained. "It's photosensitive. It can burn you, make you blind."

Wade put down his pen. He looked tired. "Did anyone go blind?"

"No, but Darlene has a rash."

Wade sighed. "Do you have this cream?"

"It got thrown out."

Wade glared at me. "Of course. You've lost your mind," he said. *Rude,* I thought. "What does face cream have to do with murder?"

"Read the news," I said. "Brian Nickerson wants Darlene to join forces with him and become deputy mayor. It's not going to happen. But if it did, she'd bring the Gasper's Cove votes with her. That would knock Elliot out of the race." Wade clicked his pen again. It was getting on my nerves. "Elliot wants to be mayor so bad he killed Mike and tried to sabotage Darlene. It's simple."

Wade was silent. He looked at the ceiling tiles, at the floor, toward the door, and through the window again. Finally, he looked at me.

"I've got a crime to solve," he sighed. "Maybe two. You have no idea what I'm up against. I don't have time for crazy talk. You don't either."

I was confused. "What are you saying to me?"

Wade was brisk. "For your information, we know where Elliot was when Mike was killed. We have witnesses. He's in the clear."

"Witnesses?" I snickered. "I can imagine. Who were they? A couple of the guys who work for the municipality?"

"No," Wade said. "*You* should pay attention to the news. There are hundreds of witnesses. Half of Gasper's Cove. Elliot was the marshal at a race at the yacht club all that day."

I had to admit that this information was a setback. But it didn't explain everything.

"What about Darlene's rash?" I asked. "What do you have to say about that?"

Wade rolled his eyes. "Look. Why don't you concentrate on the store and your arts and crafts or whatever you do," he said. "For your own good. Forget about finding Mike's killer, if you can. Forget all these silly theories, particularly the ones about giant plants. Forget anything I ever said to you about keeping your eyes open."

"That's it?" I asked, disappointed. "I'm off the case? You don't want my help at all?"

"No. Except ... " Wade sagged in his chair. He knew that he was about to say something he would later regret. But he asked the question anyway.

"There's one thing, but just one," he looked around, as if someone else who might hear was in the room. "Valerie, what can you tell me about Maud Lewis?"

CHAPTER TWENTY-FOUR

"Maud Lewis?"

Every Nova Scotian knew about our most famous artist. Little Maud Lewis, crippled by arthritis, isolated, covering her world with paint. Her tiny house was preserved in the Art Gallery of Nova Scotia. It was a national treasure. Every inch of it—the walls, the stair treads, the stove, and the kettle—was painted with what Maud saw in the world around her. Birds, flowers, dogs, and the famous black cats. The visitors who passed on the road in front of her house had noticed it. The paintings they bought had made her famous.

"I know she loved what she did," I said. "She had no choice but to create." I knew what that felt like.

I heard a door open and a voice behind me.

"Much like yourself, wouldn't you say?"

I turned around. It was Gilles. Gilles, the fancy car–driving, romantic dinner–cooking, almost-object-of-my-desires, out-of-towner with the made-up grandfather.

I gave him an honest answer. "In a way, like me."

Wade stood up and pushed a chair forward. Gilles sat down and placed some papers on the table between us.

"What I have here, Valerie Rankin, is a warrant to search your residence and place of business." His tone was formal. "We have reason to believe you are involved in, if not the leader of, a group of artisans running an art forgery ring. Specifically, one that produces fraudulent Maud Lewis art."

I looked at Wade. So that's where his question had come from.

I turned back to face Gilles and started to laugh. It began as a giggle and then got louder and more out of control. Gilles watched me, impassive. Wade was more uncomfortable and moved toward the door.

"I'll get her some water," he said to Gilles, who, I suspected, outranked him. "Excuse me."

Gilles nodded, but his eyes didn't leave my face. He sat and waited. I took a breath and wiped the tears from my eyes.

"I don't paint," I said. "I sew. I knit. I couldn't forge anything if my life depended on it." Then, the reality of the papers on the table started to sink in. A search warrant. "Hey, Toby's in the house. If your people go in, make sure that they don't let him out. Once this week is enough." I tried to pull myself together. "I don't understand. How does this have anything to do with me?"

Gilles sat back, watching my reaction as he spoke. "There are fifteen thousand fake Maud Lewis paintings in circulation," he said. "They are everywhere. Most are in private collections, but embarrassingly, some have found their way into the premier's office. Someone is making a fortune. We've watched the airports and other ports of entry for years, trying to figure out how they were getting in. Until I had an idea."

I finished for him. "They weren't coming into the country from outside, because they were being made here, weren't they?" I asked. How typically Canadian to assume that everything bad happened elsewhere.

"Exactly. Which led me to you," he said. "A local organizer of craftspeople, working in the middle of nowhere ... "

The middle of nowhere? I stopped laughing.

"Your visit to the Co-op. The dinner." I said. "You weren't one bit interested in anything except checking me out as a criminal mastermind, were you?" This was so humiliating. Why had I thought that he was interested in me? Why had I told him my whole life story and not noticed that he had shared nothing about his? All I knew was the reason he gave for being here. "What about Wade's commendation?" I asked. "The one you were supposed to be organizing? Is that made up too?"

Gilles was offended. It seemed to be okay to question the motives of everyone except the RCMP.

"Excuse me? Officer Corkum will receive an award," he said. "He's done good work, apparently." Gilles looked as though his own assessment of Wade's skills was less flattering. "The crime statistics about this community put it on our radar. It gave me a reason to come down here. What better place to hide anything than somewhere no one goes to, where no one knows about art?"

There he was again, insulting me and not having the sense to know it. Some detective.

"Right. You're more than a communications officer, aren't you? You thought you'd fooled me." He had, but indignation was replacing my sense of humiliation. "Going to check on where Granddad grew up?" I asked, pushing back my chair and standing. "Take a left, it'll take you right to Connecticut."

Gilles looked taken aback. Then, a wave of understanding passed over his face.

"You think I used you," he said. He stood up too. Our meeting was over. He opened the door for me. "I'm doing my job. I always do a good job. If our searches don't turn up anything, our investigation will proceed elsewhere. If you are not involved, you have nothing to worry about."

I picked up my purse and sailed past him to the door. I wracked my brain for a good exit line. In Gasper's Cove, high value was placed on having the last word, particularly if it was snappy.

"The veal," I said, "was tough. You used too much salt." I looked at Gilles and raised my eyebrows, giving him my best Darlene-style glare.

I was pleased to see Gilles looked as though I had slapped him.

We all have our pride.

◁○▷

After I left the RCMP detachment, I headed across the causeway to Gasper's Cove. Darlene and I had to talk, but not until I had taken a detour past my house. When I got there, I saw a dark car parked out front. I could also see Toby loose in the backyard. I was glad that both gates were closed. At least they had done that right.

With a shock, I realized that I was more offended by the presence of the RCMP searching my house than I had been by a faceless intruder in my basement. I tried to figure this out. Maybe it was because what the sign wrecker had attacked was political, not my real life. That person was likely an amateur. By contrast, the officers in the house were professionals. What were they doing? Were they going through my underwear drawer? Lifting the mattress to check for paintings under the bed? Searching behind bags of frozen peas in the freezer? Inspecting the dust bunnies under the couch? Talking among themselves, wondering why I didn't have a cleaning lady?

That was all likely. And what about the store and the Co-op? I had a message on my phone from Duck.

The feds are here? What's going on?

Duck had been incarcerated once before in his life. Police on the premises would make him nervous.

This wasn't fair. Not to me. Not to Duck. I texted back.

Nothing to do with you. Nothing to do with us. Hang in there.

Easier said than done.

CHAPTER TWENTY-FIVE

I couldn't leave Duck alone with his worst nightmare. I turned the car around and headed back down the hill to the store. Darlene and I could talk later.

I met Erin and Polly on the sidewalk in front of the doors. I looked at my watch. School was out. The girls had come to discuss their new line of headbands.

"They just left," Polly said, answering my question before I asked it. "They were like guys from a movie. I could tell by their shoes they were cops."

"She asked to see the search warrant," Erin put in.

"It was in order," Polly said. "What were they looking for? I don't think they found it. They took nothing with them when they left."

How could I possibly explain this situation to my junior crafters?

"Lost paintings," I said vaguely. I was a lousy liar.

Polly's eyes narrowed. "Whose paintings?"

I was terrible on my feet. "Maud Lewis's."

Erin rolled her eyes. "Not Maud Lewis. Mr. Ross makes us copy her paintings. He says that it's the only way we'll learn."

My head started to buzz. "Copy? What do you mean?"

"The old masters," Polly explained. "Mr. Ross says that's how they apprenticed. Like, Michelangelo copied da Vinci. I've done the oxen."

"I did the three black cats," Erin said. "Same as Sylvie's sweater, the one she's got on today."

My head was reeling. I looked down the street and saw Sylvie's station wagon. "Is she here?"

"Yes," Erin said. "She's inside, getting Duck a cup of tea." She hesitated and looked at Polly, who nodded. "Don't worry. We apologized."

"What for?" I asked.

Polly took over. "Okay. You know how you're never too young to start taking care of your skin?"

"I think so," I said. I knew the technique—a slow start to a bad story. Where was this leading?

"Erin and me, last week, we were trying out that cream. You know, the one Sylvie makes?"

I nodded.

"Maybe we didn't put the lid back on tightly ... "

"What happened? Just tell me," I said in my mother voice.

"Toby got into it. You know how he'll eat anything?" Polly asked.

"I do."

"We tried to fix it," Erin rushed in. "We went into the bathroom and got that stuff you use to clean the floors. We poured some of it on top of the cream, you know, to sterilize it. We tried to smooth it over, mixed it in a bit."

"The concentrate?" I asked, stunned. "That stuff's like drain cleaner."

"We thought we'd made it as good as new," Polly said. She paused when she saw the look on my face. "Or maybe not," she mumbled.

"Sylvie told us that you thought there was something wrong with her cream," Polly swallowed. "We told her it was probably us. She thought it was funny. I guess you don't." She lowered her head. "We're so, so sorry."

I dropped my purse on the sidewalk and leaned against a car at the curb. I looked at the girls. They both seemed ready to cry.

"Someone could really have been hurt," I said. I had accused Sylvie of something that wasn't her fault." I couldn't believe it. "You can't fix everything yourselves. It's important to know when to ask for help." I stopped. Who was I talking to? The girls or myself? A line I used with my own children came back to me. This was a time to use it again.

"You know what you call a mistake you learn from?" I asked.

"No, what?" Erin sniffed. "Tell us."

"A lesson," I said, as I had said so many times when raising my kids. "A mistake you learn from is a lesson."

Erin and Polly both nodded, subdued but relieved.

"You go on now," I said. "I'll talk to Sylvie."

As I watched the girls go down the street, backpacks touching as they conferred on their mistake, I wondered what my own lessons were.

Where did this new information leave me? I hadn't been fair to either Elliot or the Giant Hogweed. I had rushed ahead with only a theory, taking action when I should have taken pause. I owed Sylvie a huge apology. She was in the store now. I reached for the heavy door and pulled it open. It was time to show that I had learned my own lesson.

I found Sylvie and Duck in my office. They both glared at me when I walked into the room.

"Geez, Valerie. I held it together," Duck said, both hands around his hot tea. "But I'm sure that those guys knew who I was." He sank into his chair, defeated. "I heard them talking. They said 'forgery.' They meant me."

Ahh, I hadn't thought of that. I should have. Years ago, Duck's no-good brothers had given him bad bills to pass. He'd done time for it. I could see how the RCMP search had made him nervous.

I put my hands on his shoulders. "Duck, it's nothing to do with you, I promise. They're looking for art. We don't have it. We're okay."

Duck nodded, but he looked exhausted from worry. "I'd like to take the rest of the day off," he said. "I'm taking Shadow home with me."

"Good idea," I said. Shadow, Duck's gray cat, would know how to make him feel better than the rest of us could.

"Thanks." Our handyman got up, put his cup on a tray, and trudged to the door. As I watched him go, I tried to figure out how much of this was my fault.

I turned to Sylvie.

"Listen, I'm sorry," I began.

Sylvie held up her hand. "Stop. The girls already talked to me. I get it. I have kids." She took a deep breath. "I know you had to check it out, make sure everything was safe. These seaweed lotions and soaps are a new thing for me." She studied her hands. Her voice was shaky. "I try really hard."

"I know you do," I said. I hadn't expected to be the one doing the reassuring. "You've put more products in here than any other crafter."

"That's it, isn't it?" Sylvie said. "Other people I graduated with have exhibitions, they get commissions, but what do I do? A bit of everything. All I have ever wanted to do ever since school was be an artist, but I'm a nothing."

"You're not!" I needed to find the right words. I looked at her sweater. "You're like Maud Lewis. Making things, it was like ... her life-force. Look how famous she was. People pay a fortune for every little thing she ever painted." I stopped. I had remembered something, and I knew that it was important. "You said Mike told you that the *Three Black Cats* painting was done by kids. That's right, isn't it?" I asked her. "What exactly did he say?"

Sylvie looked confused, then her face cleared. "He was canvassing. He came to our door," she said. "He was interested in my sweater. We got into an argument. He said a kid had done the original. The man could be belligerent."

Yes, he could be. Scrappy Mighty Mike Murphy, forever the fight promoter. What did that autobody guy say? Mike was a man who took a cut from someone else's risk.

Then, it hit me. The RCMP didn't have two cases, it had one.

It all made so much sense. Mike was an operator to the bone. He would have managed a forger like he'd managed his boxers. They painted; he sold. But somewhere along the line, the artist had wanted out, just like the fighters had. Now, Mike was dead. I was sure that if we found who painted the fakes, we would find the killer.

I knew just where to look.

I called the RCMP detachment.

"You again?" The officer on the desk sounded tired.

"I need to talk to Officer Corkum, immediately," I said.

"Didn't you say that last time you were in here?" she asked. "He and Officer Nolan are out on police business." She paused long enough to make it clear that she didn't think that anything I had to discuss fell into that category. "Care to leave a message?"

"Yes," I said. "I need to talk to him as soon as possible."

"As ... soon ... as ... possible," the officer replied, making a show of how carefully she was taking notes.

I hung up before she did. I was in a hurry.

I took the shortcut home, past the school.

CHAPTER TWENTY-SIX

I don't know what I was expecting when I arrived at the house. I knew that it had been searched. What did they call it on TV? "Tossing the place"? Things thrown around in a crazed search for evidence. Mattresses on the floor, drawers dumped, papers scattered all over the rooms. I braced myself for the shock.

I shouldn't have bothered.

The first thing I saw when I opened the door was Toby. The second thing I saw were my shoes. They were lined up in pairs, in categories. I walked down the hall to my bedroom. The drawers in my bureau looked like Marie Kondo had arranged them. I went to the kitchen. The cans in my cupboards had been turned, label-side out.

Forget a cleaning service. Call the RCMP.

I put on the kettle and sat down to wait for it to boil. It had been a long day. I didn't have much to show for it, apart from making a fool of myself.

I needed to think about dinner. After the rich veal en papillote, I had a yearning for fish and chips, or maybe a frozen pizza. I'd eat, walk the dog, and fuse some interfacing. I needed to give my tired brain a rest.

I was just relaxing into a normal evening when my doorbell rang. I was surprised when I opened the door.

It was Catherine. A very nervous-looking Catherine.

"Can I come in?" she asked. "We need to talk."

About what? I wondered. I opened the door wide.

Catherine walked in and sat on the edge of the sofa. I could tell that she was not looking forward to this conversation.

She looked around. "I see you've been cleaning."

"I had help," I said.

Catherine reached over and adjusted the afghan folded next to her. She avoided my eyes.

"What did you want to talk about?" I asked. This visit was taking too long. I tried to remember whether I'd left the iron turned on downstairs. I still had the rest of my jacket front to fuse.

"I want to apologize," she said. "Putting Brian's sign out front was my idea. I thought it would be good for business. With the Nickerson background, I figured he'd be mayor." She shifted uncomfortably, stiff and proper on my aunt's lumpy old couch, her floral blouse buttoned right up to her neck. "I figured it might be a 'not *what* you know but *who* you know' thing."

Let me guess, I thought. *You all went to university together.*

"Why apologize?" I asked.

"I didn't mean to cause any trouble for Rollie with his family. I really didn't," she said. "I should have talked to Rollie before I let them put in the sign. I didn't. He didn't tell you that it was my fault the other day to protect me. Please don't be upset with him."

I leaned back in my chair. What was happening to me? I hadn't even voted in the last two elections. Now, here I was, letting something as stupid as a campaign sign cause trouble between myself and a cousin.

"Forget about it. Rollie and I will be fine. I understand. You were just trying to do something that was good for the Bluenose Inn." I was not in any position to comment on anyone else's mistakes.

Catherine looked relieved. "I'm doing my best," she said. "A business, having a partner, it's all new to me. I'm forty-seven years old. Everything in my life right now is a first." She paused. I was amazed to see admiration on her face. "I'm not brave like you. You know what you're doing. Fearless."

I looked at her and laughed. "Fearless? Try stupid. You have no idea the mess I got myself into today." I thought of my call to Rob at Natural Resources, my meeting with Wade, the fool I'd made of myself with Gilles.

"What mess?" Catherine asked, leaning forward. "Tell me."

For one split second, I hesitated. Then, I opened my mouth. Like the old lady on the bus who talks to the driver about her thyroid condition, like the stranger on the airplane who tells the woman in the next seat that her husband is cheating, I did something we all do at some time in our lives. I spilled my guts to someone I didn't know all that well. Because I needed to talk.

I told Catherine everything. I shared my theories about Mike's killer, I told her how Gilles had charmed me, and I repeated the debacle with Sylvie's cream. I swore her to secrecy.

I didn't leave out Maud Lewis.

"Can you say that last part again?" Catherine asked. "About the art teacher?" I was surprised that this was her only question.

"Trevor Ross has his students copying Maud Lewis paintings as an exercise." Catherine nodded, as though this made sense. I kept going. "Apparently, someone is forging Maud's art and selling it. I think that Trevor is using the kids as an innocent workforce. I think Mike saw one of the paintings at the school, so Trevor killed him."

I sat back and let myself enjoy the relief of sharing my secrets, letting all my tension go. I waited for Catherine to laugh. I waited for the ridicule. I was getting used to it.

Instead, I noticed that her cheeks were flushed and her eyes were bright.

"It sounds like a novel," she said, softly. "Mystery and detective fiction? Or would it be suspense fiction? Or maybe a thriller? It's a hard call to make."

"Excuse me?" I asked.

"Sorry. Old habits die hard," Catherine explained. "I started out at the library doing cataloging. It's how my head organizes things." Her face got even redder. "Rollie and me, well that's *contemporary romance*. The inn is 647."

"647?"

"*Hospitality and property management*. You know, Dewey Decimal," Catherine added, as if this detail was not something she should have to explain.

"Back to forgery and murder," I said. "You know the part about truth being stranger than fiction?"

"Oh, right," Catherine said. "That. Why don't you go to the RCMP?"

"I can't, not with another theory," I said. "My credibility is shot."

Catherine was on her feet now, pacing the living room, negotiating Toby's 100-pound body and the end tables.

"But what if you're right?" she asked me. "Think about it. There could be a criminal and a murderer in there with the children. We have to do the right thing."

"I told you. They'll never listen to me."

"That's because you get worked up," Catherine said. "They'll listen if it comes from someone less ... familiar. Someone more methodical. Someone with evidence."

"What are you saying?"

Catherine smiled.

"They'll listen to me."

CHAPTER TWENTY-SEVEN

The next morning, my cousin's lady friend and I were sitting in her car, across the street from Gasper's Cove Junior High.

"Tell me again. What's the plan?" I asked. Catherine's interest in intrigue had surprised me.

She passed over a paper. "I wrote it all down. Here's the itinerary."

I looked at the document in my hand. On the left was a column with the time marked in 15-minute increments, starting when the bell rang at 9:00 in the morning and ending at 3:15 in the afternoon. Lunchtime, from 11:45 to 1:00, was marked with an * and the word "surveillance." Next to the * at the bottom of the page was written, "C engages suspect, V searches site." I took this to mean that while Catherine talked to Trevor Ross, I was supposed to look for student-generated fake art in his classroom.

"Got it," I said. I thought that I would be better at talking and Catherine more efficient at searching, but I was no longer in control of this operation.

"Here"—Catherine passed me another sheet—"is the map of the premises. We are starting at the library in the northeast corner at 10:15."

"The library?" I asked.

"Our cover story," Catherine explained. "As you know, my friend is the school librarian. If anyone asks, we are in the school to help her move books. When the bell rings, we go down to the art room, against the flow of the crowd."

"That's when you charm Mr. Ross?" I asked.

"Yes. I'll get him out into the hall."

"And I sneak into the classroom and look around?"

"Exactly," Catherine said. "Remember the two Qs."

"Two Qs?"

"Quiet and quick."

"Gotcha. Anything else?"

"The code word. If Ross gets suspicious, you will hear me say '345.' Memorize it."

"345?"

"*Criminal law. Subcategory of law.*"

Why did I ask? "I think I'm ready," I said.

We stepped onto the sidewalk in front of the school.

Catherine squared her shoulders and squeezed my arm.

"Showtime," she said. "On a mission and above suspicion."

We'd see about that.

Heather, Catherine's librarian friend, was happy to see us. She had new shelving, boxes of books, and tired arms. Between the three of us, we were able to make considerable progress with general fiction, arranged alphabetically by the author's last name, and were up to M–N when the bell rang.

"Valerie's crafty. We thought we would go see Mr. Ross's art room," Catherine explained. "Maybe have a chat with him."

"Good luck with that," Heather said. "He keeps to himself. We never see him in the staff room. But he's a good worker. Always here, even evenings and weekends."

Behind Heather, Catherine wiggled her eyebrows and mouthed "345." I grabbed her and pulled her into the hallway. She had waited until the middle of her life to do something daring. She was making the most of it.

"Remember," I whispered, as we pushed upstream against a current of students heading south to the lunchroom. "This is an exploratory mission. We're here to check out an idea, not make a citizen's arrest."

"Copy that," Catherine said, which worried me. "Under control."

I shut my eyes and wished that I was at home. When I opened them, I was still in the junior high, in front of the art room.

"Trevor! What a surprise," Catherine said, dragging me into the classroom behind her. "We were just helping down in the library. I didn't expect to see you here."

Trevor pushed a stringy lock of hair behind his ear.

"I teach here," he said. "You know that."

Catherine tried again. This time, she pushed me in front of her, like some hyperactive stage mother. "You know Valerie. From the craft Co-op? She was just telling me what a wonderful job you did with the entrepreneur's expo."

This was my cue.

"I was impressed," I told Trevor. "Such talented students." I felt Catherine nudge my back. "Since we're here, I was wondering if I could see more of their work."

Trevor gave me a level look, his skepticism close to amusement. "Visitors' Day is at the end of term. Why don't you come back then?"

I'd failed.

Catherine stepped up and pulled the art teacher aside. "Actually, Trevor, that's not why we're really here," she whispered. "There is something I'd like to discuss with you. In private." She looked at me sideways, willing me with her eyes not to react. "Can I have a quick word? Out in the hall?"

Trevor appeared to be thinking hard for a reason to say no. He gave up. "I guess," he said. "If it won't take long."

"Why, thank you," Catherine said, as seductive as a woman in a cotton turtleneck and a denim jumper could be. She pushed the art teacher out of the room and closed the door behind them. "I'll be quick."

Once they had gone, I turned to the classroom.

An art room was the only place where I'd felt like I belonged when I was a kid. I inhaled the familiar smell of paint and paste, steadied my nerves, and began my search.

The big desk at the front was Trevor's. The student desks had been replaced by high tables and stools, both spotted with paint from more than one generation of junior high student. At the front of the classroom were easels, and at the back, a deep sink for cleaning up. High windows covered one wall, and a blackboard the other. The perimeter of the room was outfitted, floor to ceiling, with cupboards for supplies and student work.

It looked like any other art classroom in any junior high school in the province. But in this one, reproductions of famous Canadian paintings were taped over the entire surface of the blackboard. After my conversation with Erin and Polly, I was not surprised to see two Maud Lewis prints among these—*Three Black Cats*, the big, middle, and little cats in a row, yellow eyes wide and unblinking, and *Horses Hauling Logs in Winter*, with its blinkered Clydesdale harnessed to pull a sleigh in the winter. Maud, it seemed to me, had painted what she saw, and she saw a lot. Next to her pictures were three done by the Indigenous artist Norval Morrisseau. Like Maud's, Norval's work was clear and graphic, the bright colors outlined in black. I tried to remember something I had read about the artist. What was it?

Forgeries. The CBC had done a story. Many of the works sold as Morrisseau's were fakes. In fact, his work had been so widely copied, the artist had been forced to set up an organization just to authenticate his real paintings.

I looked at the prints. Was it possible Trevor really was at the center of a much wider forgery operation than anyone, even Gilles, had imagined?

My chest tightened. If that was true, big money was involved. A man might be killed to protect an operation of that scale. Was my librarian accomplice out in the hall with a murderer? What should I do?

Off in another part of the school, I heard the big doors open. I looked at the round clock on the wall. In ten minutes, it would be 1:00. The bell would ring, and the art teacher would be back in his classroom. I needed evidence for Catherine to take to the RCMP. I moved to the first high table. Dried paint came off on my fingers as I leafed through the first stack of curled paintings.

Sheet after sheet showed attempts, with various degrees of success, to copy the paintings at the front of the room. But each student, as would be expected, had painted their own name in the corner of the page. If a forgery ring was working in Gasper's Cove, the evidence of it was not on these tables.

The bell went off in the hall.

I looked at the cupboards along the walls. Quickly, I pushed stools out of my way and started my search. Most of the cupboards held nothing more than paint, brushes, pastels, charcoal, and different weights of paper. The last four doors were locked.

The sound of footsteps in the hallway got louder. Bumping against the tall tables, I ran to Trevor's desk. I reached for a drawer. Maybe I could find a key to open those last cupboards.

"Hey! Can I help you with something?" Trevor entered the room, Catherine close behind him. "That's my desk. What are you doing?"

"A tissue," I said, sniffing loudly. "I needed one."

"Go down to the office," the art teacher said, clearly suspicious. "I have a class coming in." He turned to Catherine. "About that other thing. I don't do those commissions. But thanks for asking." He held the door open and stood aside. It was time for us to go.

Catherine pushed me out into a stream of students.

"Did you find anything?" she asked as soon as we were outside the classroom.

"I did and I didn't," I told her. "He definitely has students copying famous paintings, but that's all I can say. Any of the work the kids have done has their names on it, and really, they don't look much like the real thing. Maybe he has the good stuff locked up."

"Exactly. Even if the kids aren't producing forgeries, that doesn't mean he isn't," Catherine said. "If not at the school, maybe at home. Anything else?"

"Yes. Tell me how you got Trevor out into the hall. What did you say to him?" I asked.

"392.5," Catherine said. "*Weddings and marriage customs.* I told him Rollie and I wanted a portrait."

"What?" I stopped on the pavement and stared. Why didn't I know about this news? "I didn't know Rollie had proposed."

"He doesn't know yet," Catherine said, with a smirk. "But he will."

CHAPTER TWENTY-EIGHT

After we left the school, I wanted Catherine to go see the RCMP.

She said no.

"A written report has more authority," she said firmly. "We have to conduct ourselves professionally."

I looked at my accomplice. No one would confuse us with professionals. "Won't writing a report take time?" I asked. What if our art teacher made a getaway while Catherine ran spell-check?

"I will prioritize," she said. "Rollie can finish polishing the silver." She seemed to be calculating the time to do the task in her head. "A draft, then a first and second edit. It should be done by dinner time."

I turned my head and looked out the window so only the trees could see me roll my eyes. "Sounds great," I said. "I'll be home. Got to take care of something else first. Call me when it's done. I won't be going anywhere." That was true. My life would be much simpler once my conversation with Darlene was over.

Darlene was zipping around her house on Flying Cloud Drive when I walked in. She had the couch pulled out and was attacking the baseboards behind it with a cloth.

"What's going on?" I asked. Darlene always did the baseboards when she was stressed.

"I'm writing a letter to the editor in my head," she explained, "to those idiots at the *Lighthouse*. I've been thinking more about all those things they wrote about you. I am so, so mad."

I threw my purse on the floor, pushed two cats out of the recliner, and collapsed into it. How was I going to do this? I got into politics because I didn't want to let Darlene down. Now, I had to get out for the same reason.

"I'm resigning," I told my cousin's backside as she crawled on all fours behind a large potted plant. "As campaign manager. I quit."

Darlene sat up on her knees and snapped off her rubber gloves. "Not accepted," she said. "We're not going to let them bully us."

"I'm doing it for you," I told her. "I was thinking about what that lady said at the meeting, about Valentine's Day. You'd be a great mayor. Me, my past, the dumb things I say and do." I thought of the new sign being put up on Sylvie's lawn. "I'm a distraction you don't need."

"But I need *you*," Darlene said. "You are my cousin. My best friend." A calculated look crossed her face. "You are like that guy in *The Loneliness of the Long Distance Runner*."

I threw myself against the back of the recliner.

No.

Not that movie.

A pseudo-intellectual older cousin had made us watch the film when we were teenagers. In it, the English underdog hero trains to run a marathon, but just before the finish line, he stops running, even though he is in the lead. Our older cousin thought that it made a statement about the integrity of individual choice. We thought that it was the dumbest thing we had ever seen. When it was over, Darlene and I threw popcorn at the TV and yelled, "You quitter!"

"No," I said. "Not at all like that. I'm Leonardo DiCaprio in *Titanic*. I am letting go of the board and sinking to the bottom of the Atlantic to save you."

"Another stupid movie, apart from the music," Darlene said. "Boards float, they would have been fine"—she gave me The Look—"like we will."

"I can't do it," I said. "I just can't. Let Annette be your manager, she'd be good at it." One of the cats jumped up onto my lap and started to purr, oblivious to the tension in the room. "I'll be the person who dresses the mayor instead. I'm better at that."

Darlene folded the spotless cloth in her hands into a neat rectangle. The baseboards hadn't needed dusting. "I know what it cost you, that stuff from your past being dragged up and the mess in your basement. I get it," she said. "But we can't give in to them."

"Why not?"

"Because that's what they expect." Darlene put her shoulder to the couch and slammed it back into place under the big picture window. "They think we're a couple of amateurs who'll fold under pressure." Satisfied with the couch's position, she started punching cushions to fluff them up. "Except I'm not"—punch, punch—"a foldable amateur."

"Maybe I am," I said. As soon as the words were out, I knew they were true. "If it's this hard to keep things the same, maybe it's time they changed."

Darlene stared at me. "I'll call Annette."

As I walked away, down the stairs, and to my car, I heard a mutter behind my back.

"Quitter."

When I arrived home, I was surprised to see the cartoon shape of the Citroën parked in front of my house. Across the street, Mrs. Smith was watching from her front yard, pretending to work on nonexistent dandelions. As soon as she saw me, she waved me over.

"Another stranger at your house," she said, stating the obvious. "Don't worry. I made sure that I could see him. And if he went around back, I was ready this time." She held up her dandelion digger. One of the tines was broken off, maybe lost in a previous defense maneuver.

"It's okay. I know him," I told her. I could tell that she was disappointed.

I crossed the street. Gilles strolled toward me. The day was warm, and the leather jacket was gone. More buttons were undone at the top of his shirt than was usual in Gasper's Cove.

"I wanted to see you again," he said. "Can we talk?"

The polite thing to do would be to invite him in for tea. I didn't offer. I wasn't sure whether that was because I didn't trust Gilles or myself.

"Sure. Talk. Why not. Why don't we walk?" I asked. I was close enough to smell his aftershave. Definitely something other than Old Spice. "Come to arrest me?"

Gilles laughed and looked up at the clouds. "I am sure you're not surprised to know my people found nothing in their search." He stopped and narrowed his eyes in speculation. "You understand, don't you? I was just doing my job. This forgery operation has taken over years of my life. It's become my obsession."

I stopped walking. I understood obsessions. I had the fabric collection to prove it. On the sidewalk opposite, Mrs. Smith was keeping pace with us, pretending to admire the neighbor's flower beds. I knew that Catherine was still working on her report, but maybe talking to Gilles would be a shortcut.

"If you wanted to know if I was running an international forgery operation, you could have just asked," I said. "I'm not. But there's someone else you should check out. The art teacher at the junior high. He's got the kids copying famous paintings. Maybe he's the master, and they are his apprentices," I added helpfully, remembering Michelangelo and da Vinci.

Gilles's head snapped around to look at me.

"When you told me about these fake paintings, it got me thinking," I continued. "I live here. If something like that is going on, I want to know about it."

Gilles was silent, as though he were translating what I had said into something a man from a metropolitan area could understand.

"I don't believe this," he said, finally. He looked over and glared at Mrs. Smith. She disappeared behind a bush. "This is my job, not yours. You have no idea who you are dealing with. Stay away from this. I mean it."

Was this concern or a warning? Something felt off-kilter, but I was too tangled up to think straight. Darlene, Catherine, Wade ... I was no longer sure when I was helping or when I was making things worse. I searched Gilles's face for clarity. It seemed to me that his eyes were even brighter in the sun. We were back at the Citroën. Gilles waited.

"I'll back off," I said. Why not agree? I was out of investigative ideas anyway. "I'll stick to what I know. Promise," I added, to end the conversation.

"*D'accord*," Gilles said, pulling his keys from his pocket. "I have to go, work to do."

Mrs. Smith and I watched him as he drove off down the hill.

I realized that Gilles hadn't asked me for the art teacher's name.

CHAPTER TWENTY-NINE

In the days that followed, Toby and I tried to return to our regular life. Maybe Gilles was right. Trying to be someone I was not wasn't working. My reputation had washed out to sea. And Emma was making sure that all of Gasper's Cove knew it.

That week didn't make me feel any better.

Monday morning, I left out a pound of butter. Toby ate it and threw up on my knitting. Tuesday, I tried to clip a stray thread on the hem but instead cut a big hole right through my skirt. Wednesday, I tried to straighten up the mop display at the store. But when I lifted the last mop, I smashed a hundred-year-old light fixture on the ceiling. Thursday, the wind broke the clothesline. A week's worth of washing ended up in the mud.

And now, on Friday, Toby and I were late for work. I hurried to the car, put Toby in the back seat, and buckled myself in. I put the key in the ignition. Click. I tried again. Click. I put my head on the steering wheel. I heard a loud doggy sigh behind me.

What did I know about cars?

Not much. I knew to put in the gas, to turn the key, and not to leave the lights on. I lifted my head and checked the lights. They were off.

Who could I call? Who would come out to help me this early? Suddenly, I had an image of a large man in overalls. I took my phone out of my pocket.

"Syd's Repairs, Autobody, and Towing," he answered. "Syd speaking."

"Hi, Syd?" I could hear the panic in my voice. "I don't know if you remember me. We met when Darlene Mowat and I were canvassing your street?"

There was a pause. "Yeah, I do, but you're wasting my time." Syd didn't sound all that busy. "I told you I don't vote."

"I know, don't worry. I'm out of that game," I reassured him. "But I'm over here in Gasper's Cove, and my car won't start. I turn the key, and nothing happens."

Syd's tone changed, relieved that this call wasn't political. "Battery? Did you leave on the lights? Anyone there who can give you a boost?" *Don't you have a man handy?* he seemed to be asking.

I looked across to Mrs. Smith's house and saw her front curtains move. "No, and I don't want to bother the neighbors. I have been having trouble with the car on and off."

"What kind of trouble?"

"It's been taking a while to start." I realized that I wasn't being much help. I tried harder. "It's like it's slowly been dying, and now it's dead."

Syd sighed. "Sounds like the starter. What's your address? I'll try to get over. Leave the car door open and the key in the console." He paused, clearly deciding he needed to spell everything out. "If I got to tow her, it'll cost you."

"That's fine," I said. Everything was costing me these days.

⌒◊⌒

Toby and I walked down to the store as fast as we could, but even then, we were late. Colleen met me as soon as we arrived.

"Elliot Carter is here," Colleen said. "I put him in your office so he wouldn't cause a scene. What did you do to him?"

I shrugged as though I couldn't imagine that anything I had done would upset anyone. I headed down to the back of the store. I was halfway there when I heard a rattle in aisle two. I looked over. Harry Sutherland was rummaging through the pails.

"Hi there, Valerie." Harry held up a red pail. "A discount? Mom's birthday."

"That sale is ended," I told him. I was in no mood. "Same price for everyone."

"Okay, I'll check the Walmart," Harry said, returning the pail to the shelf. "Listen, I heard Darlene fired you from the campaign."

I stopped walking. I'd quit. "How did you hear that?" I asked.

"Boys at the yacht club. Sarah Chisholm sent out one of those press release things, said Annette was taking over." Harry read the expression on my face and was satisfied. "It's all over the internet. Everyone is talking about it."

"That a fact?" I asked. Great. More gossip. "Whatever is best for Darlene," I said vaguely. I hoped that someone, somewhere, was recording how gracious I was.

Harry looked uncomfortable. He wasn't a mean guy, just one who didn't like to pay retail. I turned to leave.

"I wish Darlene luck," Harry said as I hustled away. "Tell her if I didn't think someone else would do a better job, she would be my first choice. And think about those pails."

With my back to him, I raised my hand and gave Harry a thumbs-up. Once again, Harry Sutherland had left me speechless.

⌒◯⌒

As soon as I opened the door to the manager's office, I knew that things had changed. The collection of empty water bottles I kept on the desk had been put in the blue recycling bin behind the door. The chronically crooked seascape on the wall behind the desk was now straight. And a quivering civil servant/mayoral candidate was sitting in my best visitor's chair.

When Elliot heard me, his white brush-cut head swiveled around.

"I could sue you for slander," he spat out. My heart sank. Wade must have talked to him.

"What for?" I asked, although I knew. I tiptoed into the office, as though to avoid the land mines I knew were there.

"I had the RCMP at my home," Elliot started to sputter, then caught himself. He pulled a shockingly white handkerchief out of his pocket and dabbed at his face before he continued. "Officer Corkum asked me about the Giant

Hogweed, of all things. Some bizarre story about face cream that he said originated with you. Have you lost your mind?"

No, I hadn't, or at least I didn't think so. But I'd let a few things slip out of that mind and fall on the floor, where they were tripping me up now. I'd meant to contact Wade and tell him that the mystery of Darlene's rash had been solved, but I hadn't. I admitted to myself that I had hoped that he'd forgotten all about it.

"Don't worry," I said. "I'll fix this. It was disinfectant from the bathroom, nothing to do with you."

Elliot pursed his lips. He sat up straight in his chair. "I'm not going to do it," he said.

"Not do what?" I asked.

"Let the craziness take over," Elliot snapped. "I watched how Mike ran things. The corruption, the graft, the favoritism." Elliot started picking golden-retriever hair off his pressed navy cotton-twill pants. "Do you know what I want?"

I didn't know, but I knew what I wanted: not to be sued and for everyone to forget every dumb thing I'd said and done so I could get back to my sewing.

"No, what?" I asked instead, to be polite.

"I want ... what I want ... " For an unemotional man, Elliot appeared to be struggling to find a way to express his deepest feeling, the heart of his soul. "I want us to be the Geneva of Nova Scotia."

"Geneva? Like Switzerland?" I stared at the man in my visitor's chair. I finally understood Elliot. He was insane.

"Yes," he said. "I want us to be so fiscally responsible, so well run, that anyone, particularly those bureaucrats in Halifax and Ottawa, will be afraid to change anything."

I was having a hard time squaring Elliot's vision of efficiency with the haphazard community I lived in. "So, what you want is ... respect?"

"Exactly. Respect on merit, not something bought with bribes, like those paintings Nickerson gave the premier," he snickered. "Fakes, just like he is." Elliot ran his fingers down the pinched peaks of the pressed creases on his pants as though the two parallel lines soothed him.

His words ricocheted around the room. Had Elliot said what I thought he said?

"Excuse me? Brian's the one who gave the premier the forged Maud Lewis paintings they found at Province House?" I asked. This changed everything.

"Yes. I was still working in Halifax at the time. Gift to the province, blah, blah, blah, said they were from his private collection, had them for years, picked them up somewhere locally," Elliot sniffed. "The fool."

This was why Gilles was in Gasper's Cove. But Mike's murder? How did that fit in? I had to get Elliot out of my office. I had thinking to do.

"Is that it? Are you going to sue me or not?" I asked, almost too overwhelmed to care.

Elliot rolled his eyes and sighed. "Darlene fired you. That's the only reason why I'm not suing, out of respect for her as a manager." He was up on his feet now, shaking out the fabric on his well-ironed legs. "But if you don't back off, and if you ever pull a stunt like that again, you won't know what hit you."

With that, Elliot pivoted and stalked out of my office. I saw that one of our price stickers, $10.99 marked down from $15.99, was stuck, with dog hair, to his rear.

I let him leave. I didn't say a word. I had other things on my mind. Like a senator's son.

◠◦◠

Aisle two was empty by the time I left the office. Harry was probably on the causeway over to the Walmart in Drummond. Colleen was at the counter when I walked back to the front of the store.

"That seemed to go well," she said as she looked out the window and watched Elliot disappear down the street. "I heard Darlene fired you. Not to worry, you're busy enough. And by the way, you've got the law waiting for you upstairs." Colleen raised her eyebrows at me. "You're a popular girl today."

"Wade?" I asked. This was all I needed.

"Wade's not the one who wants to see you," Colleen said, curious. She didn't like things to happen she didn't know about. "It's that lady RCMP officer, the one who rents Sylvie's basement."

"Dawn Nolan?"

"That's the one. You better get up there," Colleen said. "Something's up. She looked pretty worried to me."

CHAPTER THIRTY

Dawn Nolan was alone in the Co-op. She had a beach rock painted with shore birds in her hand.

"I paint too," she said.

I'd heard that. Polly said that cool things were being produced down in Sylvie's basement.

"Not creative stuff like this," Dawn continued. "I do war-gaming with miniatures. I could buy the figures and boats already finished, but I like to do it myself." She stopped, as though embarrassed by the enthusiasm in her own voice. She knew that people found her passion for toy soldiers odd for an adult, strange for a female, and unsettling in an RCMP officer.

I wasn't one of those people. Who was I to judge? DIY was my middle name. As a teenager, I had even tried to make my own shoes.

"Sounds interesting," I said, because it was. The world was full of people who made things, sometimes in disguise. I wondered what size brushes she used. "What exactly is war-gaming?"

"In my case, I like to re-create battles, but in physical miniatures," she explained. "My dad got me into it. He was a history buff."

"I understand. My father was a biologist," I said. "That's why I like the woods."

Dawn nodded. "Right. That explains the Giant Hogweed. Wade told me. He thought it was something you made up." She considered me. "You were serious, weren't you?"

"I was, and I wasn't," I said. I liked talking to Dawn Nolan. I didn't want her to think that I was crazy. "The plant is real. The sap is dangerous. But I was wrong. That's not what gave Darlene her rash." I explained about the girls and their attempt to disinfect an open jar with an industrial-strength cleaner. I had another thought. "One good thing came out of it," I told her. "Elliot Carter came to talk to me."

"How is that a good thing?" Dawn asked. Clearly, she knew Elliot.

"He told me Brian was the guy who gave the premier the fake Maud Lewis paintings," I said. "That's no small detail."

As soon as I mentioned Maud Lewis, Dawn the toy-soldier painter was gone, replaced by Officer Nolan. She reached into her back pocket, took out a folded sheet of paper, and handed it to me. It was Catherine's report, sent last night. I scanned to the bottom. Catherine had finished with "Respectfully suggest that you investigate Trevor Ross."

I pulled my eyes off the sheet. "Well?" I asked. "What did you find out? What did Wade say?" We had pointed the RCMP in the right direction. They could take it from there.

"That's the thing," Nolan said, refolding the sheet and returning it to her pocket. "We don't know where Wade is. He's gone. He didn't come in for his shift today. He's not answering his calls." She looked out the big semicircle window onto the wharf, staring hard, as though she hoped to see her partner.

"What about Trevor?" I asked.

Nolan sighed. "Ross told the other teachers he was going on a retreat." She picked up a small driftwood seagull from the windowsill, avoiding my gaze, clearly worried. "We're trying to find out where."

"Is that why you came here?" I asked. "To see if I had any idea where Wade was?'

"Exactly," Nolan said. "I wanted to know if what Catherine wrote here"—she patted her back pocket—"was based on evidence or if it was just another one of your ideas."

I swallowed. Did putting two and two together count as evidence? I didn't think so. "It was an idea," I admitted.

"I was afraid of that," Officer Nolan said. "But if you can think of anywhere Wade might have gone, if you see him ... "

"Don't worry, I'll tell him you're looking for him," I said.

"Appreciate that." Nolan let out a long breath. "His car's gone too. Not a trace. The GPS is inactive."

GPS? I got lost a lot. Darlene had threatened to have a tracking device put on my car. "What would do that?" I asked.

"Not sure. Disabled somehow." Nolan looked out the window at the ocean. "Or in the water. There's always that. If he went over a cliff and into the sea, that would shut it down."

⟨∽∘∾⟩

After Dawn Nolan left and Colleen went home, I stayed at the store to think. I went upstairs and stood at the second-floor window. Someone had left a tripod set up on the corner of Front Street. I looked past it to the horizon and the sun beginning to drop behind it out of sight. The last light of the day lit up the street like a fading floodlight. This time was not the first that a Rankin had been near trouble. We had worked with rumrunners in the old days. More than once, we had nearly gone bankrupt. But this situation was worse. No Rankin, as far as I knew, had sent a shaved-head RCMP officer off to his death. Trevor Ross was clearly dangerous. Why had we told Wade to go see him? A couple of Nancy Drews playing around like it was a game. Except it wasn't.

I wished that Dawn hadn't mentioned the water.

That's where this mess had started, when we were sitting in Wade's cruiser in the look-off parking lot, with its steep drop down to the ocean. Gasper's Cove was nothing but roads beside cliffs. Had one murder led to another? It seemed to me that if Trevor Ross had enough nerve to strangle a mayor with a tie, he would have no problem forcing an RCMP cruiser off the road and over the edge.

The Mounties would figure it out. I couldn't. The best thing for everyone was for me to go home and walk my dog. I picked up my purse, went down the stairs, and walked out onto the sidewalk. I turned to lock the doors of the store behind me.

My phone buzzed. I reached into my purse and pulled it out. A message from Syd at the garage. I read as I struggled with the old lock.

Car ready for pickup. Starter motor.

The key stuck. I tried to pull it free. My phone slid from my hand and dropped to the sidewalk. I moved quickly, but it hit the pavement hard. When I picked the phone up, I could see that the screen was cracked and dark. I leaned against the old boards of the store. What now? I was cut off. I needed to go get my car. How would I do that now?

I looked over to the parking lot of the wharf. A truck was backing out. I recognized it. I ran into the middle of the road and waved. Harry Sutherland swerved and pulled up in front of me, his two inside wheels perched on the curb.

He unrolled his window. "Hey, Valerie. How ya doing?"

"Great, just great. Huge favor. I need a lift over to Drummond to pick up my car at the mechanic's. Any chance you can run me over?"

"In Drummond, you say? I was going there anyway." Harry got a cagey look on his face. "Heard there's no good pails at the Walmart. Going to try the Home Depot ... "

I looked up at the clouds. "How about you take me over to Drummond, and I give you one of our pails, on the house?" I asked.

Harry paused, as though to run this business proposition through the crack management section of his brain. "It's for Mom. Awful big house. Upstairs and downstairs. Those stairs, hauling all that water ... "

"Two pails," I countered, "and a package of sponges."

Harry leaned over and opened the passenger door. "Hop in. Where did you say we were going to?"

I stepped up high into the truck and made a nest for myself in the pile of chip bags and old candy wrappers on the car seat. "Syd's Autobody," I said. "He fixed something called a starter."

Harry nodded sagely. "Starters are tricky. Not a job you can do yourself," he observed, as if he assumed that I would try. "I know Syd. Him and me bailed out of high school at the same time. My father didn't care, he only got as far as Grade 6, but Syd's dad was a teacher. He was some mad at Syd, I can tell you, especially since he went off and did the fights instead."

"That's right," I said. "Didn't Mike manage him?"

"Manage? Is that what you call it?" Harry snorted. "More like watch a guy get beat up and pay him peanuts. That's why I stayed out of boxing myself."

I looked over at my driver. Harry was a weedy guy, about 5′5″ if he stood on his toes, half the size of his own mother. He was hardly George Foreman material.

I pointed to the tripod on the corner. It looked to me like survey equipment someone had left behind. "Do you know what's going on there?" I asked. "Road work?"

Harry sniffed. "It's those damn developers. I know them guys. Big shots, came with Brian's dad. Nothing but trouble."

I remembered the two well-dressed men who'd come to the debate with the Nickersons. "Trouble? How?" I asked.

"My people tell me that once this town combination thing happens, they're going to come in and build a casino," he snickered.

"A casino?" I turned around to get a better look at the survey tripod as we passed. "They're huge! On Front Street? What would happen to the store?" Stuart. He was an engineer, working to get Brian Nickerson elected. Was he involved in this project? Progress and prosperity.

"They'd buy the store and flatten it," Harry continued grimly. "The island would never be the same. Those jokers would turn us into the Las Vegas of the North Atlantic. Mobsters, all-you-can-eat buffets, motels that rent by the hour ... " Harry caught himself and looked over at me. "Pardon my French. I get worked up. I had my own casino situation myself. I know the trouble they can start."

I tried to look sympathetic. Once, in his best-forgotten past, Harry had spent more money than was his at the Drummond casino. We crossed the causeway to the Drummond side.

"That's the turn," I pointed to the subdivision. "Syd's at the end of Horseshoe."

Harry crossed two lanes of traffic, oblivious to the honking. "Right," he said driving down the street and pulling up at the curb in front of the house. "Tell Syd I said 'hi.'"

"Will do," I said, sliding over the empty chip bags, my hand on the handle of the door. "You can let me out here. Thanks for the lift. You can pick up the pails tomorrow."

"Good. That will make Mom happy." Harry looked dubiously at Syd's house. Unlike the other lawns on the street, the grass here was long, wavy, and uncut. Tall weeds sprouted in what had once been flower beds. "I don't see no cars. Are you sure he's open?"

"He texted me I could pick it up. The garage is out back."

"You sure?" Harry asked. "You going to be okay?"

"Positive," I assured him. "I'll be fine."

CHAPTER THIRTY-ONE

After Harry left, I walked past the house to Syd's shop. The big doors of the garage were open. The GTO was up on the hoist. I could hear George Strait singing from a radio on the workbench. An old Ford truck and a Toyota with the side bashed in were parked in the grass to the right of the entrance. My car was on a small graveled area to the right, in a mechanic's version of an out basket, I expected.

I didn't see Syd. That disappointed me. I wanted to pay him and get back home to Toby.

"Syd?" I called out. "Syd?"

No answer.

I walked into the dark cave of the garage. He wasn't there. I went back out into the yard. On the edge of the property, I saw a shed. Maybe Syd was in there.

I picked my way along the wide, curved gravel path to the back and the smaller building. As I got closer, I could see a fender sticking out behind it. Something about the fender looked familiar. I widened my circle to get a better look. I stopped walking. That wasn't a car back there. It was a lot more. It was an empty RCMP cruiser.

Behind me, I heard the gravel crunch.

Before I could turn around, Syd walked in front of me. "Come for your car?" he asked, wiping his hands on a greasy rag.

"Yes. Thanks for fixing it," I said.

"I'll grab the keys. Be right back." Syd looked at the partially hidden RCMP vehicle, then back at me. He disappeared into the garage.

As I waited, I studied the shed. Now that I was next to it, I could see that it was larger than I thought, narrow at the front but running long into the back of the yard, as though it had been built for some specific purpose. The windows were small, with mismatched frames, all undoubtedly salvaged. The thick steel door, with its rivets around the edges and elaborate locking system in the center, looked like it had come from a meat locker. Whatever was in that shed was worth protecting.

Why would anyone put an industrial-strength door on a ramshackle little building at the end of a backyard? The rest of the property seemed so neglected. A row of overstuffed trash cans had been left between the garage and this building. Crows had ravaged the black plastic bags they held, and cardboard boxes from frozen dinners, beer bottles, and empty baked-bean cans were now fanned out over the overgrown grass. I kicked away a flutter of aluminum foil as it drifted across my feet, its edges fluted with tiny zigzags, blown by the wind from the direction of the cruiser. I stopped, bent down, and picked it up. It was the wrapper from a stick of Juicy Fruit gum.

The back door of the garage banged open, and Syd emerged. He held up my key chain. "Here you go," he said. "Cash or check would be fine."

I took the keys but didn't move.

"Where's Wade?" I asked.

CHAPTER THIRTY-TWO

"What are you talking about?" Syd moved closer to me.

"This RCMP cruiser." I walked over and tapped the hood with my hand. "What's it doing here?"

"Doing a little work on it," Syd said. He flattened his face, removing all expression.

"Work? Like disabling the GPS?" I knew that might be a dangerous thing to say, but I said it anyway.

At the mention of the GPS, Syd looked both ways, as if he were expecting an interruption. He took another step closer. I could smell bacon and beer on his breath. I felt sick.

My fear made me giddy. "Wade's missing," I continued recklessly. "So is his car, and the car's here. What did you do with Wade?"

Syd ignored my question. "Did he send you?" he asked. "This is about my dad's paintings, isn't it?" Syd had a large heavy wrench in his hand, one of the adjustable ones. I hoped that he wasn't thinking of adjusting me.

His father? Paintings? Random facts rattled around my skull. I struggled to chase them, to slow them down, to make them tell me what this meant. I took a chance.

"Your dad was an art teacher, wasn't he?" I asked. "When Trevor Ross was in school."

"Trevor who?"

I took another leap. It was time I learned something solid. "Trevor wasn't the forger, your father was. It was your dad who did those fake Maud Lewis paintings all these years." It made sense to me now.

Under the dirt and grease deep in his pores, Syd's face went pale. "I was right. The big boss sent you. The one who organized everything." He said it as a statement of fact. The heavy wrench went back and forth from one hand to another. I tried not to watch it. "I've got to put you away with that cop. I need time."

I felt cold. "The killing's got to stop," I argued. *Before you get to me would be a good time to retire*, I thought. "Don't kill me. Not like Mike, not like Wade." I tried to reason with him. "You can't keep doing this. It's going to catch up with you."

"Mike?" Syd asked. "That was an accident. He was doing that door-knocking thing. He walked right into the shed and found me finishing a couple of pictures. Some of the ones Dad didn't get to before he died. Mike said he knew a buyer, someone trying to impress his old man. He bought them from me." Syd tightened his grip on the wrench. Shame and despair were in his eyes. "I'm an idiot," he said. "Do you know that?"

Actually, I did. The idiot part didn't worry me, but the possibility of a dangerous idiot did. I felt that the moment called for diplomacy.

"Let me get this straight. Your dad was an art forger, and you finished his work after he passed?" Syd nodded. "Seems reasonable. And you gave the paintings to Mike to sell?" It was a crazy story. I also felt that an important part was missing. I just wasn't sure what it was.

"Mike took a cut, just like he did when I boxed," Syd said, almost pleading with me. "I watched my dad do those pictures out here for years. I thought that I could do it just as good." Syd slammed the wrench into his palm so hard, I thought it would break. "But I blew it. My stuff looked fake. Someone in Halifax noticed. Mike tried to blackmail me. He said that he was going to tell them who done the paintings." Syd looked to me for understanding. "Him dying, it was an accident."

I remembered the tie. That Windsor knot didn't look like an accident. It looked like a whole lot of rage. Crazy person rage.

"But Wade," I persisted. "Why kill him?'

Syd looked shocked. "Kill an RCMP officer? Are you nuts?" he asked, as though I was and he wasn't. "Do a thing like that, and they hunt you down for sure. The Mountie's in there," he said, gesturing to the shed. "You can keep him company."

Something inside me dropped. Was this how it was supposed to end? Me locked up with a bald-headed Mountie in a shed behind an autobody shop, left to fade away? I had to keep this maniac talking. Anything to keep him from locking me up and throwing away the key.

"You asked who sent me," I said. "I'll tell you—no one. I came here to pick up my car. That's it. Why are you so afraid?"

Awareness passed across Syd's face, and with it panic. He knew that he had made a mistake, that he had told me more than he should have. He regretted it, and the shame made him aggressive. He lunged for me. The grip of his meaty hand on my arm hurt. He slammed me toward the door of the shed and held me there. He fumbled to punch in a code. The door opened. Syd threw me inside. The door slammed behind my back.

The room was dim, illuminated only by the light working its way in through the few tiny windows. It took a minute for my eyes to adjust enough for me to see where I was.

The interior of the shed looked to me to be a workspace, once used and now deserted, a place where things were made and stored. The air was stale and smelled of mice and mold. I saw fungi growing quietly along the bottom of the windowsill. I heard water somewhere dripping onto the cracked concrete floor. It was not a place anyone would stay in long, not unless they were locked in, a double-thickness industrial metal door standing between them and an outside, healthier world.

I looked for an exit, a way to escape. One side of the room was occupied by a chest-high workbench, scored with decades of saw cuts and dried confetti-like bubbles of paint, with cast-iron vices screwed to its lip. The other side wall was completely covered in $2'' \times 4''$ supports, built like outsized tray racks to hold what looked like precision-cut stacks of plywood and plywood boards. Below the racks, the floor was littered with plastic milk cartons. These held twisted snakes of extension cords, spent caulking guns, rusted and empty turpentine cans, and crusty brushes stiff with old paint.

The end of the space was covered by a blue tarpaulin attached with three-inch nails to the joists that crossed the rafters of the ceiling. For a crazy moment, I had hope that on the other side of this tarp might be another door, or a window, that would let me get out of this place. I pushed the stiff plastic aside.

Beyond the curtain was another tarp, but this one was on the floor. On it was a large water-stained bundle of pink fiberglass insulation, its cotton-candy edges ragged with sawdust and dead insects. Propped up against the bundle was a slumped and battered shape, wearing the uniform of the Royal Canadian Mounted Police.

I had found Wade Corkum.

CHAPTER THIRTY-THREE

"Wade!" I said, squatting down. "You're not underwater!"

Wade looked up and tried to focus. "Valerie?" He shifted. "What are you doing here? Water?"

"We've been looking for you. Me, the RCMP. We thought maybe you had taken a header over a cliff."

Wade mumbled, but I couldn't understand his words.

I looked around. Near us, on the floor, was a lightbulb in a metal cage attached to a long extension cord. I saw an outlet low on the wall. I plugged the light in and held it to Wade's face. He squinted at the glare, but not before I could see his eyes. I was no nurse, but they didn't look right to me. One of his pupils was large and black, and the other one wasn't. This was not a good sign, I knew that. Wade had to get to the hospital, and fast.

"How are you feeling? What happened?" I tried to keep my voice calm.

Wade struggled to sit up. I could see that he was hurt.

"I did what you said. I went to see that teacher, Ross." He slurred when he spoke. "He told me he had the kids copy pictures because that's what the guy who taught him did," Wade winced. "He said it was old school, but it got the kids working."

"I know. Syd's dad was the teacher."

"Yeah. How did you know that?" Blood from a gash on Wade's head had trickled down and gone black above his eyebrows. "I figured I should come out and talk to Syd about his father. Maybe give DeWolf something"—he hesitated, embarrassed—"to impress him."

I leaned back. "Let me guess: Syd thought you were on to him. That's why he did this to you."

Wade nodded uncomfortably. "I wasn't expecting it. I didn't move fast enough. He hit me with a wrench, threw me in here." He paused. "My car still out there?"

"It is," I said. "He's moved it back so you can't see it from the road."

"He took my gun and my keys." The shame seemed to hurt Wade more than the pain.

"We've got to get out of here," I said, gently, not sure how we would do that. Wade grunted and closed his eyes. Was he going to pass out on me? What should I do? I tried to dredge up memories of Girl Guide first aid. All I could think of was to keep him talking and, I hoped, conscious.

I talked. I told Wade that anyone could have lost their car, gun, and keys. I told him about my children, and then, when I was sure that he wasn't listening, I told him about the parchment heart Gilles had made and the muffins Stuart had baked. I talked and talked, listening for a response, straining to hear his grunts, worried when those faded away. Eventually, I, too, went silent and, leaning against the dirty roll of insulation, fell asleep until the noise of banging outside woke me.

It was Syd. He seemed to be working his way around the perimeter of the shed, knocking something heavy against its sides.

Then, the smell hit me: gasoline.

Syd was going to burn us alive.

I grabbed Wade by the shoulders. "Can you get up?"

Wade reached both his hands out wide and put one on my shoulder and one on the wall of the shed. He pulled himself up to a shaky stand. He looked behind me blankly, like he had gone someplace else in his mind. I wasn't sure whether he knew who I was. He was scaring me.

"Hey, Coach," he said. "What's the play?"

My mind raced. This was going to be harder than I thought. The smell of gas was as strong as the locked metal door that was trapping us inside. I had to come up with a plan.

"I know it's asking a lot, but if I can get that guy to open the door and get past him, I could get out on the street." I tried to think of all the possibilities. "Get help."

I wasn't sure whether Wade heard me. He was swaying where he stood, with blood coming out of one ear.

The banging outside continued. I tried again.

"If I escape, I need you to stop him from coming after me. Can you do that?" I asked Wade. Of course he couldn't—this was hopeless.

Wade opened his eyes and looked at me. "Defense," he said, removing his hand from my shoulder and holding himself steady. "You need me to play defense."

I didn't know what he was talking about. "Can you help me?" I asked again.

"No big deal to play hurt," Wade tried to smile. "Don't worry, Coach. I'll keep the front of the net clean."

The noise outside stopped.

I moved to the locked door. My enforcer, who I was sure was hallucinating, staggered close behind me.

I smashed my fist on the door.

"Syd," I yelled. "I lied. I know who the man at the top is. You'll never see him coming."

Silence. *Oh boy*, I thought, *he's looking for matches.*

"You do, do you?" Syd shouted back, but I could hear the fear in his voice. "Tell me who he is, or you both go up in flames."

"No deal," I screamed at the door. "Do you think I'm stupid? If I tell you, you'll burn us anyway. There's a guy in here hurt, probably dying." Through his fog, Wade looked startled. I shook my head. "An RCMP officer. That's big trouble. You know that."

"Who is the boss?" Syd repeated. "Dad wouldn't tell me."

I was making progress.

"Like I said, put me on the other side of this door and we'll talk. You let me live, and I'll give you time to get away." What else could I say? "He's already on to you," I continued, ad-libbing. "You're out of time." That was it, my whole negotiation repertoire.

Silence.

"Yeah, maybe I don't want no cop to die on me," Syd said. It seemed to me a bit late for him to worry about other people, but I let that pass. "You tell me who the man in charge is. Then, I'm going to lock you in a car, put you up on

199

the hoist. That will give me time. I'll let them know where to find you."

This idea seemed to me to be the stupidest I had ever heard. Up on the hoist? But with Syd's decision-making track record, I wasn't surprised.

"Deal," I said, nodding to Wade. Amazingly, he had found an old hockey stick leaning against the wall. It was in his hands now, the ragged tape hanging off the blade in dusty ribbons.

The handle on the outside of the door jiggled. A sliver of light appeared along its side.

This was my moment. I sent up a silent prayer to all the Rankin women in the past who had, at various times in their lives, dealt with impossible situations and unreasonable men. *I need you now. Everything you got*, I whispered to them.

I began to move toward the door, but before I got there, Wade slammed past me, knocking me out of his way with a shoulder, charging ahead.

The door flew open.

Then, with the old hockey stick high in his hands, Wade barreled straight through the door, shrieking like a warrior from another world, from the past. It was the scream of our Highland ancestors, the same ones who had been on the battlefield with William Wallace, the same ones who had gone over the top at Vimy Ridge. It was a battle cry revived and recovered by an RCMP officer who had once almost been drafted by the National Hockey League. Out through that door, like a primal locomotive, Wade charged. In an instant, he had his hockey stick right across Syd's throat, smashing the mechanic up against the wide-winged fin of the 1957 Chevy parked in the yard.

This was my moment.

With my protector defending me, I skated past them and out to the safety of Horseshoe Crescent. Somewhere behind me, I heard Syd choke out a last threat: "You'll never get away."

But I had.

CHAPTER THIRTY-FOUR

I was saved by a quart of milk.

This is the story, as much as I can make sense of it.

It all started with Harry's mother. She had been getting ready to make bread pudding at around the same time Wade and I had been locked in the shed, awaiting incineration. Halfway through her preparations, Mrs. Sutherland realized she needed milk.

When he heard this, Harry, who loved his mother's bread pudding, volunteered to run over to the Foodmart and pick some milk up. There at the checkout, he ran into Stuart Campbell. Harry and Stuart got to talking, and while they watched Mona ring them up, Harry noted that this trip to Drummond was his second of the day. The first was when he'd dropped me off at Syd's garage.

This fact interested Stuart. He told Mona and Harry that he had been trying to reach me all day. He had something on his mind, but my phone wasn't picking up. Mona said that this was odd. Leaving together, Stuart and Harry decided that I must not have plugged it in. They both knew how distracted I could be.

Later that day, Colleen showed up at the Foodmart. She needed tomato paste because her spaghetti sauce was no good without it. Chatting with Mona, Colleen asked the cashier whether she'd seen me around because I hadn't shown up at the store. Mona replied no but added that Stuart couldn't find me either. Thinking aloud, Colleen wondered whether I was over at Sylvie's, apologizing for the Giant Hogweed fiasco. Mona agreed that this might be a possibility. Polly had told her mother the whole face cream story. Polly's mother was Mona's cousin's husband's sister.

After she left the Foodmart, Colleen called Sylvie. Sylvie told Colleen that I had already apologized, sort of, but agreed that it was odd no one knew where I was. Sylvie then went down to her basement apartment to talk to Dawn Nolan, who was getting ready for her early shift. Dawn, who was still worried about Wade, decided that one missing person was enough. On her way over to the detachment, Dawn decided to swing by Horseshoe Crescent, the last place I had been seen.

She arrived just when I needed her.

I was beginning to think that the professor at St. Xavier University knew what he was talking about.

$$\sim\!\!\!\int\!\!\!\sim$$

The first thing Dawn did when she arrived was to call an ambulance. She shouted that order into her radio as she ran across the yard to pry Wade off Syd and handcuff the mechanic's meaty hands behind his back. Two more RCMP cruisers arrived soon after. This backup was a good thing because it took three strong officers to get Wade into the ambulance. Even then, they were not able to get him to give up the hockey stick. I heard later that the technician who took the pictures diagnosing Wade's concussion had suggested that the next time Wade played road hockey, he should wear a helmet.

It turned out that, like me, once he started talking, Syd didn't know when to stop. He told the RCMP how hard it had been to be a painter of cars when his father was a painter of art. He told them how sorry he was that twice in his life, he had allowed Mike Murphy to get him into trouble. He even admitted that he had been the inept forger of the paintings in the premier's office and explained the route that got them there.

Shortly after Syd's arrest, Brian Nickerson withdrew from the mayoral race. Apparently, he remembered that he needed to spend more time with his family. As a result, Brian closed up his campaign office, as well as his summer house, and went back to Halifax. Senator Nickerson returned to Ottawa soon after. Brian's sister had decided to run in a by-election there, and the senator thought that he would give her a hand.

Emma left town with him. Her rhyming-title hit jobs in the *Lighthouse Online* had impressed the senator and his staff. As a result, she was offered a job on his communications team, which she accepted. We all agreed that Emma had a great future ahead of herself in the nation's capital.

Emma's departure put Noah back on the general news beat, including municipal affairs. I assured him that nothing exciting would ever happen again in the community and that he could still concentrate on sports. That suited him, and it suited me.

I hoped that I would never see my name in print again.

CHAPTER THIRTY-FIVE

Darlene won the election. All of Gasper's Cove got out to vote, but the turnout in Drummond was confused. One candidate had been murdered, and one had left town. It didn't matter. The best woman won. Amalgamation was stopped in its tracks.

The morning after the election, we decided to hold a press conference in the parking lot of the Drummond Interpretive Center where it had all begun. It was a clear and fresh Nova Scotia day. The breeze seemed to be blowing our way.

The crafters all came early and helped me set up. We borrowed a podium from the center and arranged the plastic chairs around it. Darlene had chosen her own outfit, a periwinkle dress, coral shoes, and matching beaded earrings. Colleen was there, too, all dolled up and installed as mother-of-the-mayor at the edge of the parking lot in her own one-person receiving line. The first hands she shook belonged to Trevor Ross, who arrived looking rested and serene. The RCMP had found him in a Buddhist retreat down in the valley.

Stuart came, too, with Erin and Polly, who had worked together on Darlene's speech. When we were waiting for the rest of the crowd to assemble, he ambled over to me, working his way slowly through the crowd.

"Have a minute?" he asked. "There's something I want you to know."

"Sure," I said, wondering what he had to say to me now.

"Glad this is over," he began, looking at the water instead of at me. "How about you?"

"You can't imagine," I replied. "It was like a fever we all caught."

"You got that right," he said. "I try to get along. I try to take care of people. My clients, at home with Erin. This ridiculous fake conflict, the politics, pretending it mattered, just about killed me. Plus, I spent most of my time worried about you."

"Me?"

"You and Darlene are tight. We all know that," he said. "So, I wasn't surprised you were working for her. But look what happened. You found Mike, you almost get killed yourself out there at Syd's." Stuart swallowed hard and put his hands in the pockets of his jeans. "And then, when they went after you in the news, I just lost it."

"You did? How?"

"First, I went official. I filed a formal complaint with the Canadian Journalist's Association. Then, I left a hundred crazed messages for the publisher."

I smiled to myself. No wonder the *Lighthouse*'s mailbox was full.

"I wanted you to quit, so you would be safe," Stuart said. "It's the worst feeling in the world to want to help someone but not know how to do it. Particularly when they are as tough as you are."

I wasn't sure whether this was a compliment or not. I could figure that out later.

Stuart wasn't done.

"That's not everything. After someone was in your house, I went over and talked to your neighbor—you know, the one who lives across the street." Stuart looked at me with one eye closed, as if gauging my reaction with caution.

"Mrs. Smith?"

"That's the one," Stuart said. "I gave her my number. I told her if she saw anyone around the house again to give me a call."

He must have made Mrs. Smith's day. No wonder she spent so much time hovering behind her curtains.

It was my turn to share.

"About those signs that got trashed. There's something I haven't told anyone. There's no point now," I said, looking over at Noah. "This was told to me in confidence."

"You can tell me, you know that," Stuart said, but he looked worried.

"It was her, you know, Emma, that young reporter." It made me angry all over again to think about it. She'd admitted it to Noah. "She wanted something dramatic to write about, so she went into my house and broke the signs." Stuart stared at me as I continued. "And that X on the wall? She thought that it was like a mark on a ballot. She wanted to make it look political."

"You are kidding me. Look what she put us all through! How scared you were ... " Stuart looked more upset than I had ever been. "I hear that she's going to be working with the Nickersons. She'll fit right in."

The bitterness in his voice surprised me. "What do you mean?" I asked.

"You weren't the only one who quit as campaign manager," Stuart said. "I tried to call you. Tell you the day you went missing. It didn't matter after that."

"What do mean you quit?" I pointed to Stuart's hand. "What about the ring? The roommates?"

Stuart laughed but without humor. "Forget about the ring. You got it all wrong." He leaned closer to me, our faces inches apart, like two co-conspirators. "You got involved because you believed in Darlene. I got mixed up in this election because I felt I owed Brian for something that happened a long time ago."

"Owed him?" I asked. "For what?"

"I thought he did me a favor once," Stuart said. He shook his head at the memory of his younger self. "He and I were so different. I was a nerd, the guy with the student loan. I was never one of the cool kids."

The wind off the water ruffled Stuart's dark hair. His sailor's eyes, creased by the weather, had seen more voyages than I knew. "Well, you're cool now," I said.

"Thanks," Stuart smiled at me, then his face turned grim again. "University was different for Brian. He had this ability to make doors open. I'd watch him. I'd never seen anything like it."

"The senator's son," I offered. "It's like his middle name."

"Exactly," Stuart agreed. "When we graduated, it was the same. He articled for the biggest law firm in Nova Scotia. I don't even think that he applied."

"And you?"

"I sent out application after application to everywhere I could think of. It was tough. You remember what the economy was like then."

"I do. What happened?"

"Well, one day, out of the blue, I got a really good offer from a terrific firm." Stuart looked over my head at some memory only he could see. "I couldn't believe how lucky I was."

"I am sure you worked for it."

"Yeah, anyway, when I told Brian, he smiled and said, 'I had a word with my dad.' I remember it. That was exactly what he told me."

"I understand," I said. "The senator pulled some strings for you, so when Brian needed help, you felt you couldn't say no. Am I right?"

"You got it," Stuart shook his head. "Anyway, a couple of weeks into the campaign, I got the senator alone. I wanted to thank him, you know, for doing what he did for me when I was starting out. And guess what?"

"What?"

Stuart moved closer. Our shoulders touched. "The senator had no idea what I was talking about. He didn't even know I was an engineer." Stuart looked sideways at me, to make sure that I understood.

I did but couldn't believe it. "You mean, you got the job on your own merit, and Brian took the credit?"

"Yes, that's exactly what happened. And he let me believe he got me my first job for all these years."

"What a sleaze." It was all I could think to say.

"Tell me about it," Stuart said. "Why do you think I voted for Darlene?"

∞

I was still pondering Brian Nickerson's character when Darlene stepped up to the podium and tapped on the microphone.

"Thanks for coming, folks. And thank you for electing me mayor," she began, beaming at the crowd. "I know you voted for me because you know who I really am. And I know because of that, you will understand what I am going to say next."

My cousin searched for my face in the crowd. We made eye contact. Behind me, I heard Elliot Carter clear his throat. Darlene looked out at the familiar faces in front of her and then over at the waves in the bay. She put her notes down on the podium.

"I don't really want to be mayor," she said. "I had a vision for keeping our communities intact. I had something in my heart. I thought this was the way to express it. I was wrong."

Darlene had everyone's attention now. Noah drifted in closer, his reporter's eyes alert.

"The thing is, politics doesn't work the way life does. It makes everything a fight. It pretends that some people are all right and some people are all wrong." She paused to let that sink in. "We all know that's not true. We're each a bit of both." The audience went silent. Not one person there disagreed with her.

"So, who's going to be mayor?" a man from Drummond called out.

"The very close runner-up," Darlene said. "The right man for this job, the way it needs to be done. Elliot Carter."

All heads swung to look at Elliot. He struggled to smile.

Darlene wasn't finished.

"Knowing him as I do, I can tell you this: Elliot is a man with no vision."

Somewhere out in the crowd, Harry Sutherland clapped.

"And that is exactly what we need. Elliot will make sure our roads are cleared in the winter. He will guarantee that the garbage will be picked up on time. He's a man who will notice the potholes, who will get salt on the sidewalks when it's icy. When the rest of us are asleep in our beds, he's the guy who'll stay up late working to make sure we get value for every last cent of our tax dollars. Elliot is a man who will do all the worrying so the rest of us don't have to."

The crowd applauded, it seemed to me with relief.

Darlene stepped aside and motioned to the now-empty podium. "Elliot, over to you."

The crowd parted to make way for their new mayor. Elliot bounded up to the podium.

"Thank you, Darlene," he said, nodding to her and then turning to the people assembled on a beautiful day. "I want to share with you the results of the discussions that led us both to this point."

We went quiet.

"First," Elliot held up one bossy index finger, "there's going to be a change in official titles. I'm dispensing with 'Your Worship.' Just call me Elliot."

There was applause.

"Right on, brother," Harry Sutherland shouted, enjoying himself, breaking the tension with laughter.

"Second," Elliot held up two fingers to the crowd, "the Office of Deputy Mayor will be renamed the Office of Administration for the Town of Gasper's Cove. That job is Darlene's."

Sylvie Kulberg stood up and whistled. The other crafters rose to their feet as a unit and gave this a standing ovation.

Elliot almost smiled, then raised his hand again. "Third, we will have a new municipal department, the Office for the Protection and Preservation of Coastal Wildlife. Charlie Landry has graciously agreed to head this new agency."

Kenny MacQuarrie, with a platinum-haired Annette right beside him, cupped his hands and called out "About time." Charlie stood up, took a bow, and sat down, as happy as I had ever seen him.

Elliot wasn't done. "Finally, and most importantly, Miss Mowat and I propose that our two communities amalgamate municipal services, but *only* those services," he said with emphasis. "Roads, infrastructure, things like that. In all other areas, we have decided the two towns should continue to operate as distinct entities."

The crowd roared.

I realized I had been holding my breath and let it out. There we had it. A commonsense solution, arrived at only when every other option had been exhausted. We were going to do what we should have done anyway, after having paid the price of one strangled ex-fight promoter, the partial disgrace of one chicken sweater–knitting anarchist, and the transportation of an autobody man to a provincial jail.

Looking over the water to Gasper's Cove this all seemed to prove that all the cunning and corruption in this world could never undo, or re-create, a true Nova Scotia original. Maud Lewis would have agreed.

CHAPTER THIRTY-SIX

A week later, we had a second ceremony. This one was not held on the water with a view but in front of the RCMP detachment, on a patch of grass between the front door, the parking lot, and a row of shrubs.

Unlike Darlene's communal event, this one was staged for the cameras. It was dominated by a big city official who said that he was here because his wife wanted to see this part of the country. He began his speech by explaining to all assembled how much he loved lobster, sailboats, and salmon fishing. He then handed Wade a framed certificate, almost as an afterthought.

To her great credit, and against protocol, Dawn Nolan then asked whether she, as Wade's partner, could say a few words. Hearing this question, those who had pulled their keys out of their pockets, ready to leave, sat back down in their seats.

"Starting with the North-West Mounted Police, they always said the Mounties always got their man," she began. Dawn was nervous when she started speaking but soon gathered steam. "It sounds good, but it's not easy. It takes someone with real character, an officer like Wade Corkum, to come through like that. Officer Corkum plays it by the book, right to the end, whatever it might cost him, whoever might try to stop him." She stopped to take a breath, to give herself a minute. "We're lucky to have him serve." Nolan glanced sideways at her superior officers. "That's all I have to say. Wade deserves this award," she finished, as though defying anyone who thought otherwise.

The brass looked at each other. I had heard that there was talk of promoting Wade to a position outside the region and relief at HQ when he declined. He belonged here, and his partner knew it.

The small crowd dispersed, but Noah remained. Ignoring the officials from Ontario, he pulled Wade into a corner and hauled his recorder out. The headline of the article he would later write read:

Hockey Legend and Hero Cop Escapes Death in Time for Outstanding Duty Award
A Lighthouse Exclusive Interview

Noah got it. A good reporter always does.

$$\sim$$

After I left Wade's ceremony, I decided to go for a drive to clear my head. Two official ceremonies in one week were more than enough for me.

I headed out along the coast. My car ran smoothly. I was glad that Syd had fixed my starter before his arrest.

I wasn't far down Shore Road, right at the look-off, when I saw the parked Citroën. Cutting across traffic, I pulled into the U-shaped drive and stopped next to it. Gilles was there, with his back to me, looking out at the ocean. He turned when he heard my car and walked over.

"Hi," I said. "I've come from Wade's ceremony. I thought you'd be there."

"Not my job anymore," he said. "It's over, after all these years. I thought it was going to fade away, but now it's really done."

He wasn't talking about the job, I realized. "You mean your investigation of the forgery operation?" I asked. "Did you have any idea it would turn out like this when you came down here?"

Gilles smiled at me and touched my face with the knuckles of his right hand. He didn't answer me directly.

"Last year, we got word from Europe that the supply had dried up. It had been a long career, and we assumed that whoever the forger was, he ... or she," he said with a nod to me, "had died."

"Then, what brought you here?" I asked.

"Ah, Nova Scotia," he sighed. "Such a small place and always so much trouble."

"What do you mean?"

"Those two paintings at Province House. Two," he looked irritated, as though just when he'd thought his neat case was wrapped up, it had unraveled. "The curator from the Nova Scotia museum said that parts of both paintings had been done recently by someone new. He could tell by the paint and how it was used." His face told me that Gilles viewed this new information as an irritant. "I had to deal with it."

I didn't understand what he meant. "Brian told everyone he'd owned those paintings for a long time. He lied?" I had never warmed up to Brian. I had been somewhat disappointed he hadn't been arrested for art fraud. However, he'd been caught out in a lie. At least that was something.

"Of course, he wasn't telling the truth," Gilles shrugged as though this was to be expected. "But I can tell you it's a rare thing to get a confession before you've asked the first question. He was quick to tell us where the paintings came from. He was only trying to emulate his father."

The story of his life, I thought, and a sad one. "It was Mike who sold him the art, wasn't it, not Syd?" I asked. "That's what started all of this."

"Yes," Gilles said. "But we didn't know that at the time. I came here to find out who had done these two paintings. It would have saved me so much trouble if Mike had been alive when I got here."

I thought of the afternoon the RCMP had cleaned my house. "If you had been able to get to Mike, then you wouldn't have searched the store or where I lived, would you?" Somewhere in the back of my mind, my intuition was waving her hands, but, as usual, I ignored her.

"Yes, I apologize." Gilles nodded to me deferentially. "At the time I was trying to identify this new painter, whoever it was who was trying to get in on the action." Gilles tightened his jaw. "It was the one last loose end to be tied up in Gasper's Cove before I left."

"Left?"

"Yes. I am retiring. That's why I wasn't at the award ceremony. Before this trip, I told my bosses that when this art fraud case was closed, I was done." A fleeting moment of wistfulness passed over Gilles's handsome face, then disappeared. "My departure will be expected."

"Where will you go?" I asked.

"I have many places I can be," he said. "You do too. A woman like you could be someone, go places."

I looked at him. The sun was about to drop below the horizon out over the sea. When it did, it would take this day with it.

Toby was waiting for me at the store. We were overdue for his walk.

"I already am someone," I said. "I already am someplace."

There was a silence, broken only by the sound of the gulls. Gilles studied my face, as though he were searching for something that wasn't there. Then, he sighed and, with one last glance at the water, walked away. I watched him open the door of his strange car. He started the engine. The suspension inflated, slowly lifting for take-off to places I'd never see.

Gilles turned to me one last time and lifted his hand. What I thought would be a wave turned into a salute.

Then, he was gone.

CHAPTER THIRTY-SEVEN

When I got back to the store, Toby wasn't at his usual post in his recliner at the front.

"Upstairs," Colleen said. "Rollie's down in plumbing, and Toby went up to the Co-op with Catherine." This made sense. If Catherine was here, Toby would follow her. Catherine never stopped by without a few dog biscuits in her pocket.

Toby was behind the counter, working his way noisily through the treat, when I got to the top of the stairs. Catherine was near the window, counting napkins. She stopped to pick up a bar of Sylvie's soap, sniffed it, and put it back down.

She looked up at me, excited.

"Guess what?" she said. "It's all coming together. The bookings for next season are rolling in. The Buddhists say we are on the right median for meditation, they're giving us three weekends. Someone from Scotland is coming over with his girlfriend to make a surprise proposal. A company from Drummond wants to come for their monthly meetings. And we've got weddings, at least three."

Weddings? I raised my eyebrows, but Catherine shook her head. Rollie didn't yet know that he was engaged.

"I am here because I want to know about your dates." Catherine held up a large bound book. "Put it into the calendar. For that crafter's retreat you were talking about."

I had almost forgotten that idea. The crafters and I had talked for months about holding a summer retreat for our visitors where we could teach sewing, quilting, knitting, and jewelry-making. This scheme had been our big idea for the next stage of the Co-op and our little island, long before we had let ourselves be detoured by politics.

Catherine waited for me to say something.

I tried to reel my mind back to where it had been months ago, to those plans. "The second week in August? Does that sound right?" I asked.

Catherine put down her pen and picked up a pencil. "You tell me, it's your event. How about I write you in for now, and you can let me know for sure?" She plunked down a stack of napkins on the counter. "We're going to need these."

"Will do," I said. I picked up Catherine's credit card and tried to assemble my thoughts. The retreat. Should we do short project-based workshops or something all day? How much should we charge? How many students per class? Did the inn have enough electrical outlets for sewing machines? How could I ask some of the crafters to teach and not the others? We needed a meeting. I would contact Sarah and have her put the word out.

The sun broke through the clouds and sent planes of light through the window and onto the ancient floors of the Co-op.

The life I knew had returned, closing over me as though I had never left it.

~~~~

Later that night, Dawn Nolan dropped by the house. I had just bent down to pick up a bag of muffins Stuart had left on the steps when I heard her car pull up.

"Toby and I are going for a walk," I said. "Want to come?" I put the bag in the mailbox and picked up Toby's leash.

"Love to," she said.

We went our usual route, down the street past the Smiths', across the playground of the school, and up near the path that led to Charlie's house. Dawn didn't say much. We talked about dogs, and I told her about the retreat. She said that if we did any painting, she might come. She was wondering whether she should try to do something larger than miniature soldiers. I told her that the agenda hadn't been set, but I'd let her know.

When our circuit was complete and we were back at the house, Dawn lingered. I had a feeling she still wanted to say something to me.

I lifted the lid of the old mailbox. "Stay for a muffin?" I asked. Dawn smiled and sat down. For a while, we sat there together, the three of us, and felt the soft end of the day on the breeze.

"Funny thing," Dawn said, breaking our companionable silence. "They found an abandoned car in the parking lot to the Newfoundland Ferry, up in North Sydney."

I waited. You didn't rush Dawn.

"Québec plates. An old car," she added.

"Let me guess," I said. "It's his, isn't it? He's the man at the top, the one Syd was afraid of?"

"Looks like it. I have some friends in the Royal Newfoundland Constabulary. If he's there, the RNC will let us know."

"If he's not in Newfoundland, where would he go?"

"St. Pierre and Miquelon, I'm guessing. To France. That's where most of the forgeries done here ended up."

It made sense. The two islands were only an hour and a half by ferry off the coast of Newfoundland, and they were still, after all these years, part of France.

"You think that's it? His escape route?"

"It's a possibility," she said, rubbing her hands so the crumbs fell on the grass. "It was a complicated operation. He was a complicated man. I wouldn't be surprised if we never see him again."

After Dawn left, Toby and I stayed on the steps, just as I had on the night I had waited for him to come home. The big dog leaned against me, maybe remembering too. We looked up at the moon and then at each other. Leaving the last muffin on the bottom step for the raccoons, we turned and went inside.

⌣ THE END ⌣

READER'S GUIDE

Crafting Deception
BY BARBARA EMODI

1. Many readers have said that they wish they could visit Gasper's Cove. If you were doing an ad campaign for Tourism Nova Scotia, what line would you use to attract tourists to Gasper's Cove?

2. Did any of you look up Maud Lewis and her paintings after reading this book? Do you like learning more about Nova Scotia arts and crafts in this series?

3. Darlene runs for mayor. Do you think that it is still harder for women to get elected?

4. The author has worked for politicians in various elections and as a journalist. She brings that experience to this book. Was there anything about the process of running for office, or reporting on it, that surprised you?

5. In this book, Valerie notes that the pressure of public life, even in the setting of a small town, has the potential to make a person start acting the way other people expected, but that the real power lies in remaining who you are. Do you believe that this is true? Can you think of a time when you found yourself acting out of character because you were in the spotlight?

6. Darlene's story is about a local woman trying to keep her small community from being absorbed and turned

into just another bland town. We have all seen those "donut towns," everything on the edges and empty in the middle. What do you think can be done to revitalize small town centers?

7. Valerie has done a lot with her life since her return to Gasper's Cove, but something is still holding her back. What is it?

8. Were you surprised at the arrival of Gilles DeWolf in Gasper's Cove? Do you think that he will reappear in Valerie's life? (Author's note: DeWolf might seem like a dramatic name for this character, but it is my sweet mother-in-law's maiden name, and yes, she is from Isle Madame. I thought that she would enjoy seeing it in print.) If you were to cast Gilles DeWolf in the movie version, which actor would you use?

9. Valerie believes that, in a way, she and Stuart Campbell are headed to a shared future. She notes, "I had started to feel that we were like two small boats, sailing in parallel, hulls briefly touching, but somehow headed to the same port." Do you think that he feels the same? If Stuart is really interested in Valerie, what should he do next?

10. What do you think about Wade? Do you think that he is a hero or not? What do you think that he needs to learn about himself now?

11. Do you think that Darlene's decision not to accept the position of mayor is the right choice or a mistake? Why?

12. In this book, Valerie and the crafters continue to struggle with people not taking them seriously or seeing the value in creativity. Valerie even asks, "Who had decided

that working with your hands was less significant than working with your head?" Do you agree with Valerie that as a society, we devalue creativity and manual labor? If so, how do you think that can be addressed?

13. Stuart confides to Valerie, "It's the worst feeling in the world to want to help someone but not know how to do it. Particularly when they are as tough as you are." Have you ever felt powerless to help someone you cared about? How did you overcome the issue?

14. Gilles tells Valerie, "A woman like you could be someone, go places," but she answers that she already is someone and is someplace. What do you think that this exchange says about both Gilles and Valerie? Do you believe that it sheds any light on Valerie's development since she moved back to Gasper's Cove?

15. Which was your favorite scene in the book, and why?

16. Which secondary character would you like to know better? If you were to write a story about them, what would happen?

17. In the next book, *Crafting a Getaway*, someone will find love, and someone will lose it. Can you guess who?

ABOUT THE AUTHOR

Barbara Emodi lives and writes in Halifax, Nova Scotia, Canada, with her husband, a rescue dog, and a cat, who all appear in her writing in various disguises. She has grown children and grandchildren in various locations and, as a result, divides her time between Halifax and  the United States so no one misses her too much.

Barbara has published two sewing books—*SEW: The Garment-Making Book of Knowledge* and *Stress-Free Sewing Solutions*—and in another life has been a journalist, a professor, and a radio commentator.

YOUR NEXT FAVORITE

quilting cozy or crafty mystery series is on this page.

Want more? Visit us online at ctpub.com